THE SECRET ELEPHANT
OF HARLAN KOOTER

THE SECRET ELEPHANT OF HARLAN KOOTER

DEAN HARVEY

Illustrated by Mark Richardson

HOUGHTON MIFFLIN COMPANY

BOSTON 1992

Library of Congress Cataloging-in-Publication Data

Harvey, Dean.
The secret elephant of Harlan Kooter / Dean Harvey : illustrated
by Mark Richardson.
    p.   cm.
Summary: Harlan, a young resident of Pine View, Florida, tries to
hide an escaped circus elephant.
ISBN 0-395-62523-8
[1. Elephants — Fiction.   2. Friendship — Fiction.   3. Florida —
Fiction.]   I. Richardson, Mark, ill.   II. Title.
PZ7.H267475Se   1992   91-45955
[Fic]—dc20   CIP
                                        AC

Printed in the United States of America
VB 10 9 8 7 6 5 4 3 2 1

This Book Is For Elephants Everywhere

THE SECRET ELEPHANT
OF HARLAN KOOTER

CONTENTS

· 1 ·

THE GREATEST SHOW IN PINE VIEW

This is a story about a boy named Harlan Kooter. Harlan lived in a town called Pine View, Florida, where he was the smallest boy in his school. Pine View isn't very big itself, and to tell you the truth, there aren't a lot of pine trees there—just a few small, scraggly ones that haven't grown much since the day they were planted. The town is mostly a lot of sand and scrub grass, and the houses in it all look like cracker boxes someone set on their sides and cut doors and windows out of. The best thing about Pine View is that it sits next to the Atlantic Ocean, so there's always a sea breeze passing through it.

Pine View has a post office, a school, a firehouse, a gas station, and the Pine View Diner, where Harlan's mother worked as a waitress. Harlan's mom made barely enough money to support them, so as soon as Harlan was old enough he took a paper route to help out.

Being the smallest boy in school wasn't easy for Harlan, and his hair made it even worse. Harlan had the reddest hair anyone had ever seen, and as much as he tried to comb it down flat it kept sticking up in little spikes all over his head. Everybody at school teased him about it. Monica Jeebers, a skinny girl with pigtails and a turned-up nose, would squeal at him on the playground: "Spider mite, spider mite," which is a tiny red creature so small it can hardly be seen.

The biggest boy in school was a bully named Mickey Fungo. He used to steal Harlan's lunch and call him Carrot Kooter. Harlan would go after him like a little hornet and try to get his lunch back, but Mickey Fungo would laugh and hold him off with one big hand, and with the other hand he'd eat Harlan's sandwich. Harlan didn't have much chance to grow bigger with Mickey Fungo eating his lunch every day.

Harlan's life might have gone on like this forever, but it didn't. Things happened. And some of them made his life more difficult than it was already.

Everything started one Thursday morning when Harlan crashed his bicycle. He was pedaling home after delivering his newspapers when he swerved to avoid a fat raccoon waddling across the road. Harlan went into a ditch and fell off the bicycle. After he picked himself up he noticed his chain was broken, and he knew he wouldn't be riding again until he had saved enough

money for a new one. He could deliver his papers
without a bike, he thought, but it sure wasn't going to
be easy. He walked the bicycle home and put it in the
garage.

The next morning Harlan got up extra-early, slung
his big canvas newspaper bag over his shoulder, and
left the house on foot. It was still awfully dark out.
There was a breeze blowing off the ocean, and the cold
seeped into Harlan's clothes. He thought about his

nice warm bed with the big, colorful quilt on it, and how wonderful it would be to snuggle down into it and snooze cozily until the sun came up and it was time to go to school. All he had to do was call the newspaper and tell them his bicycle was broken and he couldn't make his route anymore. But Harlan knew how badly his mom needed the money he made. So he zipped up his jacket and started walking to the newspaper office.

When Harlan arrived at the *Pine View Sentinel,* the stars were beginning to fade in the sky. Soon the sun would come up, and shortly after that it would be time for school. He had to hurry. Mr. Cheever, the man who distributed the papers to the newsboys behind the long brick building in which the *Sentinel* was written and printed, was surprised to see Harlan so early. He was a cheerful, friendly man with almost no hair on his head. He was carrying newspapers out of the building and stacking them up for the newsboys when Harlan came walking up into the light. "Well, Mr. Kooter," he said, "what brings you here at this hour?"

"I wanted to get started early on my route," Harlan said.

Mr. Cheever nodded. "Where's your bike, son?"

Harlan told him about the chain.

Mr. Cheever scratched his bald head. "Are you planning on delivering your papers on foot, Harlan?"

"Yes, sir."

"But, Harlan," Mr. Cheever said, "that's miles of walking. And those papers are heavy."

Harlan stretched to his full height, which wasn't much. "I can do it."

Mr. Cheever shrugged. "Well, Harlan," he said, "it's up to you." He helped Harlan roll up his newspapers and load them into his canvas bag.

Harlan usually rested his bag of newspapers on the handlebars of his bicycle, but now he slung it over his shoulder. Harlan was so small the bag hung almost to the ground, and the bag was so heavy it tilted him sideways.

Mr. Cheever looked at him doubtfully. "You don't have to do this, son," he said softly. "Nobody would blame you for giving up now."

Harlan looked up at the graying sky and acted as though he hadn't heard what Mr. Cheever had said. "I better get going," he said. "It's almost light." He shifted the load on his shoulder a little and tried to stand up straight. "So long, Mr. Cheever."

Mr. Cheever stood and watched as the little redheaded figure hurried off into the dawn.

Harlan started out as quickly as he could, but it didn't feel at all like he was carrying a bag of newspapers. It felt like a load of rocks instead. It was almost a mile to the first delivery on Harlan's route, and by the time he got there he was so tired he wasn't sure he could go on.

Whack! Whack! Whack! Harlan started throwing papers left and right. His route was over a mile long, but halfway through it his bag started to feel lighter, and soon he noticed he wasn't bent over anymore. He started to pick up speed. Toward the end of his route he was trotting steadily along, not even slowing down to throw. And then he reached into the bag for another paper and there wasn't one. He was done. He had made only one mistake on the whole route, when he accidentally threw a newspaper through an open window and a cat screeched inside. Every other paper had landed properly on a front porch.

Harlan had no time to rest. School was starting in a few minutes, and to get there before the bell rang he was going to have to run all the way.

Harlan ran and ran and ran, with the big canvas newspaper bag flapping behind him like an old coat. He thought he might make it if he kept his head down and his legs moving. The town was awake now, and in the morning light streaming in from over the ocean, even the little cracker-box houses looked pretty. Harlan didn't slow down to admire them. He just kept running as hard as he could.

The first period bell was ringing when Harlan reached the school. He opened the front door and raced through the empty halls with all the strength he had left. He reached his room just as the bell stopped ringing, and slid quickly into his seat.

The whole class turned to look at Harlan gasping and panting at his desk. Even his teacher, Miss Honeycutt, a prim old woman with hair pulled back in a bun, took a good look at him.

"Well, Harlan," Miss Honeycutt said with a smile, "I'm glad you could make it. You know we all hate to start without you."

Half the class tittered quietly, and then Miss Honeycutt turned and walked to the blackboard.

Monica Jeebers, who sat right next to Harlan, leaned his way and whispered, "Spider mite, spider mite," and stuck out her tongue. Normally Harlan would have made his most hideous Halloween face back, but today he was too tired to care.

At recess Mickey Fungo lumbered up to Harlan on the playground and stood in front of him with his arms folded. Being the biggest boy in school, Mickey knew that Harlan couldn't ignore him when he was standing there.

"Well, carrot-head," said Mickey, "where's my lunch?" He meant Harlan's lunch, of course, which he had stolen so many times now that he had come to think of it as his own.

"I don't know where yours is," Harlan said, "I left mine at home." That was true. Harlan had forgotten to take his lunch out of the refrigerator when he left the house that morning.

"That wasn't nice," Mickey said, with a chubby-faced smile, "I wanted to eat it." A group of children gathered around, waiting to see what would happen. Mickey winked at them. "Carrot Kooter forgot my lunch."

"No," Harlan said patiently, "*my* lunch."

Mickey ignored him and kept talking to the other children, especially Monica Jeebers, who was always his best audience. "I think I ought to teach carrot-head a lesson," Mickey said, "so he doesn't forget to bring it tomorrow." He grinned wickedly at Harlan, pushed him down and sat on him.

Mickey was so heavy that Harlan thought he would be squished like a bug, but after a while he found he could breathe a little. He couldn't turn his head much, but out of the corner of his eye he could see that Monica Jeebers was laughing at him.

"Well, carrot-head," said Mickey, "are you going to remember to bring my lunch tomorrow?"

Harlan was too flattened to talk, and he couldn't think of anything smart to say anyway.

Mickey picked a blade of grass and started tickling Harlan's face with it. "Now, tell me, Kooter. Did you really forget your lunch, or are you just too poor to have one?"

Harlan tried to turn his face away from the grass but couldn't. Finally he scrunched up his face and closed his eyes, and then Mickey gently guided the blade of grass up Harlan's nose and tickled it around. Monica like that so much she jumped up and down and squealed.

"Tell the truth, Harlan," Mickey said. "It's because you're poor, isn't it?"

Harlan opened his mouth to say "Nope" and then clamped it shut again.

Mickey kept right on tickling the inside of Harlan's nose. "It's because you're poor, I'll bet. You're probably too poor to go to the circus this weekend."

Harlan's eyes slowly came open. "What circus?" he asked, in a thin, panting voice.

Mickey grinned down at him. "You didn't even know, did you? A circus is coming to town. They're going to set it up in the big field along Citrus Street."

Harlan tried to act as though he didn't care about some old circus, but the truth was, he cared a lot. He had always dreamed about going to one, and now, lying squashed beneath the weight of Mickey Fungo, he instantly imagined all the wonderful things that he would see there. There would be tents, of course, enormous ones bigger than houses. And inside the tents he would see clever white horses that could sit down on their hind legs and wave to the crowd with their hoofs. There would be dancing bears, and miniature dogs that leaped bravely through hoops of fire. The crowd would gasp as high above them trapeze artists spun across empty space and caught each other at the last possible moment.

But the best part of a circus, in Harlan's opinion, was something else entirely. He could barely talk, being mashed the way he was, but he had to ask Mickey Fungo one question. He looked up at Mickey, opened his mouth and gasped, "Elephants?"

Mickey looked down at him scornfully. "Of course they have elephants, Kooter; it's a circus." Then Mickey leaned down closer. "You know what else they have, carrot-head? A price of admission. Wanna guess what it is?" Harlan didn't, so Mickey told him anyway. "It's five dollars to get in."

Harlan was stunned. Five dollars? Where would he get five dollars? He started to feel like he was sinking right into the playground.

Mickey saw Harlan's reaction and smiled wickedly. "You don't have the money, do you, Kooter? I'll tell you what, though. If you remember to bring my lunch in, I'll tell you all about the circus on Monday.''

The bell rang, signaling the end of recess, and Mickey got off Harlan and went inside. Harlan lay there for a few moments, not wanting to move, but finally he got up and slowly walked back into school.

More than anything in the world, Harlan wanted to see that circus. He thought about it for the rest of the school day, and all the way home that Friday afternoon. Harlan had never been to a circus, but he was ready to bet it was the best thing there ever was. By the time he got home, he knew that *somehow, someway,* he had to get in.

Later on, as Harlan was eating his supper, he tried to think of a way to earn his circus money. He gave everything he made from his paper route to his mother, so that was out, and anyway, he wouldn't be paid again until the beginning of the week. By then the circus would be gone. He had to make the money before Sunday night.

Lying in bed that night, Harlan had an idea.

The next day, Saturday, Harlan had to help his mother around the house. But early on Sunday morning, he went next door to his neighbor's house and knocked on the door. A minute later a thin, white-haired man swung the door open wide. It was Tennyson Smith.

"Well, well," the old man said with a smile, "it's Harlan Kooter."

Mr. Smith was once a farmer in Iowa, but when he got old he moved down to Florida, where it was warmer. He never shaved very well, so there were usually odd little tufts of bristly, white whiskers sprouting from his chin. But he was a friendly old man and Harlan liked him.

"Good morning, Mr. Smith," Harlan said.

"Good morning yourself, Harlan," Mr. Smith said. "What can I do for you?"

"Well, sir," Harlan said, "I was wondering if I could mow your lawn."

Mr. Smith scratched his chin. "Mow the lawn, eh? Well, now, I don't know."

Mrs. Smith came out from the kitchen. She was a small round woman who was always baking cookies and pies and chocolate fudge brownies. "What is it, dear?" she asked Mr. Smith.

"It seems that Mr. Kooter here has gone into the lawn-mowing business," Mr. Smith said.

"Why, hello, Harlan," Mrs. Smith said. "What a wonderful idea."

"Hello, Mrs. Smith," Harlan said.

Mr. Smith scratched his chin some more. "Well, I don't know, Harlan. How much money would a superdeluxe lawn-mowing job cost?"

Harlan swallowed. "Five dollars," he said quietly.

Mr. Smith whistled and looked at Mrs. Smith. "Imagine, Emma. Five whole dollars."

"Well, dear," Mrs. Smith said, "this isn't 1937. You can't get it done for a quarter anymore."

Mr. Smith scratched his chin and looked at Harlan shrewdly. "Well, Harlan," he said, "I think five dollars for a lawn-mowing is mighty steep, but here's what I'll do for you. Do you know where Mrs. Smith's sister lives, over on Conch Street?"

Harlan nodded.

"Harlan," Mr. Smith said, "if you get over there and mow her lawn after you do ours, I'll give you five dollars for the pair."

"Now, Papa," chided Mrs. Smith, "that's a lot of work for Harlan."

"I can do it, Ma'am," Harlan said. For five dollars to go to the circus, he also would have washed their car, cleaned their kitchen, and vacuumed their whole house.

"Well, then," Mr. Smith said, "shall I get the mower out of the garage for you?"

But Harlan was already on the way. "No, sir," he called over his shoulder. He pulled open the garage door, pushed the little red mower out from where it was resting in the shadows, and hauled on the starter rope. The engine started with a mighty roar.

It wasn't easy for Harlan to push the mower around the Smiths' yard. He was so small that he had to reach up to grasp the handle, and that made it difficult to put his weight into pushing. But Harlan didn't care. It was a bright, sunny day, the grass made a sweet smell as he cut it in long, straight rows, and he was on his way to the circus.

About halfway through the Smiths' yard, though, Harlan noticed that something was happening. As he cut the lawn, little bits of old dry grass were getting thrown up into the air by the mower. And some of these little bits of dry grass were settling in his hair. Worse than that, some of them were slipping down the back of his neck and under his shirt. It started to get very itchy in there. The sun was getting hot.

When Harlan finished with the Smiths' yard he didn't take a minute to rest. He wanted to make sure he earned his five dollars before he stopped working. So he just shut off the mower and pushed it over to Mrs. Potter's house.

Cutting Mrs. Potter's lawn wasn't much different from cutting the Smiths'. The dry grass kept drifting down Harlan's shirt, and he kept getting hotter and hotter, and itchier and itchier. He kept pushing, though, without taking a rest. He was going to see those elephants no matter what.

It took Harlan an hour to mow Mrs. Potter's lawn, and when he had finished he pushed the mower into the street and trotted along behind it. He wanted to get back to the Smiths' and collect his circus money.

Harlan picked up speed as he turned up his own

street and saw the Smiths' house. He raced up their driveway as fast as he could push the mower, forgetting all about how hot he was and how much grass had fallen down his shirt. He tucked the mower into the garage, carefully shut the door, and hurried up the walk to the house.

When Harlan reached the door he saw an envelope taped to it with his name on it. They must not be home, he thought, and they left the money for me here. He tore open the envelope and found a note inside. This is what it said:

Dear Harlan,

Mrs. Smith and I were very pleased with the mowing. You should be proud of a job well done. We are going fishing for the rest of the weekend, and when we get back tomorrow we will pay you the five dollars.

Your good friend,

Tennyson Smith

P.S. If we run into some good catfish, we'll bring you one.

Harlan was stunned. Tomorrow! The circus would be gone by then. Why hadn't he told them he needed to be paid today? He put the letter in his pocket and walked slowly over to his house.

When Harlan's mom got home from the Pine View Diner that night, she thought Harlan had the flu. He looked pale, he didn't want to eat anything, and he seemed very, very tired. She took his temperature, and even though it turned out to be normal she sent him to bed anyway. Harlan lay there wide awake for a while,

thinking about the circus elephants. They had probably all walked up into the big red trucks by now, and were rumbling along the highway on their way to another town. Harlan wished he could have seen one of them, just one, up close. But before he fell asleep, he decided Mickey Fungo was right. He was just too poor to ever get into the circus.

· 2 ·

WHAT THE CIRCUS LEFT BEHIND

Late that night, something woke Harlan up. He didn't know what it could have been, for as he lay there in his bed, it seemed to him that Pine View had never been so quiet. The air outside his little house was so still he couldn't even hear the palm trees rustling. It was as though the entire earth had stopped turning and hung motionless in space.

But then, as Harlan began to drift back to sleep, he heard a noise outside the house. It was not a *loud* noise, but somehow it seemed to be a *big* noise. Or no, that wasn't it, thought Harlan, it sounded like a *quiet* noise made by something *big*. Something *very* big.

Whatever was out there, Harlan didn't like the sound of it at all. He scooted down into the middle of his bed and threw the covers over his head.

Harlan felt safe in the darkness under the covers. If the enormous thing outside managed to get into the house, it would have a hard time finding him. But when Harlan tried to go back to sleep, he couldn't.

His curiosity was eating at him. And as much as he tried not to think about it, he just had to know what was out there.

Harlan threw off the covers and lay there for a moment with his heart pounding. Then he got up and walked quietly through the house to the kitchen. There was a flashlight in a drawer by the sink, and he took it out and went to the door.

Harlan opened the door slowly and stepped outside. It was very dark out, but he didn't turn on his flashlight. He quietly closed the door behind him and stood in the driveway, listening. At first he heard nothing. And then, very close to him, something moved.

Harlan snapped on the light, but there was nothing to be seen. He played the light all over the driveway and still couldn't find anything. It was very strange, because whatever had made the noise sounded very big.

Then Harlan heard the sound again, behind him. He spun around and his flashlight beam caught . . . the garage. Whatever it was, it was in there.

Harlan walked up to the garage door very slowly, and the closer he got the less he wanted to open it. But he bent down anyway, and took the handle in his hand. Then he heard the noise again.

Harlan let go of the door handle and stood up. He didn't really want to know what was in there, he decided. It would probably be gone by morning anyway, so why bother? He turned to walk back into the house.

But something stopped him. He stood there in the darkness and whispered to himself. "Chicken. Chicken, chicken, chicken." He slowly turned back and bent over to grasp the handle. He took a deep breath. Then, with a mighty pull he ripped open the door and shone his light into the garage.

What he saw amazed him. Right there, in his own garage, was an elephant. At least Harlan *thought* it was

an elephant. All he could see was its rear end. But it was the biggest rear end he had ever seen. And it had a little elephant tail on it.

The elephant, or whatever it was, was really crammed into the little garage. Harlan wondered for a moment how it had managed to stuff itself in there. It wasn't making any sound at all. It just stood there silently.

Harlan cleared his throat. "Ahem," he said, but there was no reply. He tried again. "Excuse me, are you an elephant?"

There was a long silence, but Harlan waited patiently and finally the reply came from inside the garage. "Yes."

Harlan was thrilled, although he didn't know what to say. He had never met an elephant. It was clear to him, though, that this was the perfect opportunity. "Good evening," Harlan said politely. "My name is Harlan Kooter."

Harlan waited again, but the elephant made no reply. "What's your name?" Harlan asked. After a long time, the elephant said something quiet and muffled that Harlan couldn't understand.

Harlan didn't want to be pushy. First of all because he believed in politeness, and second of all because it wasn't often you got to meet an elephant, and he didn't want to offend this one. On the other hand, the elephant *was* in Harlan's garage, and it *was* the middle of the night. The elephant at least ought to say what his name was. Harlan didn't think this was a rude sort of an elephant, though. He had a strong feeling that this elephant was just very shy. The thing to do, Harlan decided, was to be friendly but firm.

"Mr. Elephant," Harlan said, "I'm very glad you like my garage. Would you come out, please, so I can meet you?"

There was another long pause, and then something that sounded like a sigh, and then the big, gray elephant began to back slowly out of the garage. In a few moments he was out in the driveway, and he turned to face Harlan.

"Hello," said Harlan.

"Hello," said the elephant.

After that Harlan just looked at him for a while. He decided right then and there that nothing was so terrific-looking as an elephant. He could see right away that this was not a full-grown elephant, but neither was it a baby elephant. It was a medium-sized elephant, which is to say it was about the size of a delivery van. It had big floppy ears; wrinkly, leathery skin; and a long trunk that reached almost to the ground. On both sides of the trunk were curved white tusks. His eyes were dark and had big wrinkly lids around them.

"My name's Harlan Kooter," said Harlan. "What's yours?"

"Hannibal," said the elephant in a very quiet voice.

"Where did you come from?" Harlan asked.

"From Africa," said Hannibal the elephant.

Harlan scratched his head. "Well, how did you get here?"

Hannibal sighed. "I came with the circus."

"The circus?" Harlan said. "But they left town tonight."

"I hope so," Hannibal said.

"Wait a minute," Harlan said. "You mean you ran away?"

"No," Hannibal said, "I just stayed behind."

Harlan didn't see what the difference was. It seemed to him you were either with the circus or you weren't.

"Well," Hannibal said, "are you going to call the police?"

Harlan wasn't sure what he should do. He couldn't understand why anyone would leave a circus once they were able to get into one. Maybe Hannibal had done something wrong. He seemed like a perfectly well-behaved elephant, but how could you tell?

"Why did you stay behind?" asked Harlan.

Hannibal was silent for a long time. And then he spoke so softly that Harlan almost didn't hear him. "Because," Hannibal said, "I wanted to be free."

Harlan stood quietly with the elephant for a long moment, thinking what he should do. "You don't have to go anywhere," he said finally. "You can stay at our house."

Hannibal seemed to perk up when he heard that. His big ears lifted and rustled by the side of his head, and his trunk curled up and gently felt around Harlan's face. "Really?" he asked.

"Sure," Harlan said. "You can stay in the garage. Say, do you want some cookies?"

"I like cookies," Hannibal said, and Harlan ran into the house to get some.

As Harlan was climbing up on a chair to get the cookies out of the kitchen cabinet, he started asking himself some questions. How was he going to keep an elephant hidden in his garage? Would the circus come looking for Hannibal? What would he feed him? An elephant must eat an awful lot, thought Harlan. And most of all, what would he say to his mom?

For the first time, Harlan was glad that his mother couldn't afford a car. Not having one, she hardly ever went out to the garage. Of course, when the moment was right, he'd tell her about the elephant living there, but the right moment might not arrive for a while.

Harlan looked at the kitchen clock as he scrambled down with a bag of cookies. It was getting late. Soon he'd have to go out on his paper route. He was halfway to the door when he had a wonderful idea.

Standing in the driveway again, Harlan opened the

bag of cookies and reached in for one. He held it out for Hannibal, but the elephant's trunk dipped quickly and delicately into the bag and came out holding a cookie of its own. The trunk curled down between the curved ivory tusks and placed the cookie in Hannibal's mouth. Then the big gray elephant trembled for a moment. "Lemon wafer," he said. "My favorite."

"Hannibal," Harlan said, "have you ever been on a paper route?"

Hannibal didn't answer. His trunk arced up, darted lightly into the cookie bag, and came out with another lemon wafer. The cookie quickly disappeared into his mouth.

"Most kids do their routes on bicycles," Harlan said, "but mine is broken right now."

Harlan couldn't tell if Hannibal was listening. The elephant's trunk was moving quickly and gracefully between the cookie bag and his mouth. Back and forth, back and forth, went Hannibal's trunk.

"I was wondering," Harlan said, "if you could help me with my route this morning."

The elephant kept dipping his trunk into the bag until the last cookie was eaten. He didn't seem to believe there weren't any left. His trunk rummaged around in the empty bag for a while, and then gently plucked it from Harlan's hand and turned it upside-down. When nothing came out the elephant dropped it.

Harlan picked up the bag and wondered where elephants learned their manners. "Well," he asked Hannibal, "do you think you could help me? With my paper route, I mean?"

Hannibal rustled his big floppy ears. "What's a paper route?"

Harlan explained and asked Hannibal again if he would help.

"O.K.," said the elephant.

Harlan went inside and got his big canvas newspaper bag. When he came out and looked at Hannibal, he realized there was a problem. How would he get the newspapers onto Hannibal's back? And how would he secure them up there? He stood in front of the elephant, trying to figure it out.

Suddenly, the elephant's trunk circled Harlan's waist, and before he could cry out it lifted him high in the air. In the next instant he was upside-down, then right-side up and settling gently onto Hannibal's back. The powerful trunk released him and the elephant began to move.

It was magical to be riding on Hannibal's back. Although it would be morning soon, it was still very dark out. The stars were shining above Pine View, and a light breeze was coming from the ocean. The elephant glided through the quiet, moving so smoothly that Harlan couldn't tell when one step finished and the next one began. Perched behind the elephant's head he was far above the ground, but somehow he felt safe and secure up there.

Harlan guided Hannibal through the streets toward the *Pine View Sentinel*. When they were a block from the newspaper, Harlan stopped the elephant and asked to get down. Hannibal's trunk curled up and circled Harlan's waist, turned him over in midair, and gently set him on his feet.

Harlan didn't know how Mr. Cheever would respond to his arriving on an elephant, and besides, until he knew whether anybody was going to come looking for Hannibal, he thought he'd better keep him a secret. "Wait here, Hannibal," Harlan said. "I'll be back soon."

"Where are you going?" Hannibal asked. He sounded anxious.

"Don't worry," Harlan said. "I'm just going to get my papers. I'll be right back. Wait here, O.K.?"

"All right," Hannibal said.

Harlan hurried down the street toward the *Sentinel*. When he got to the end of the block he turned to make sure Hannibal was still waiting. Instead, he found the elephant following three feet behind him.

"Hannibal," said Harlan, "please! Until we find out if the circus is coming back for you, we have to keep you a secret. Now, *please,* wait right here."

"O.K.," Hannibal said, and Harlan hurried off.

Mr. Cheever was behind the *Sentinel,* and he smiled when Harlan came trotting up. "Hello there, Mr. Kooter."

"Hello, Mr. Cheever," Harlan said. "Are the papers ready?"

"They're just coming out now," Mr. Cheever said. "What's the hurry?"

"I'd like to get my route done early," Harlan said. What he didn't say was why. He was just realizing that he had to get every paper delivered before it was light out. If he didn't, someone was bound to see him riding around on Hannibal. He quickly rolled up his newspapers, stuffed them into his bag, and hurried off.

Mr. Cheever watched him go, smiled, and shook his head. "That Harlan," he said, "he's a real mover."

When Harlan got back to Hannibal, he found the elephant waiting patiently where he had left him. Harlan hugged his bag of newspapers to his chest so they wouldn't spill out, and Hannibal hoisted him up and set him on his back.

"We've got to hurry," Harlan said, "or somebody's going to see us." They moved quickly through the darkened streets of Pine View, the elephant's padded feet making no sound. Then they reached the beginning of Harlan's route, and he started throwing his papers.

The paper route was easy with an elephant to ride. It was even better than having a bicycle. Harlan didn't have to pedal and throw at the same time, and the view from the elephant's back was much better. All he

had to do was pull the papers out of the bag and sling them onto the front porches as the elephant strode past. It was much faster than doing the route on foot.

They weren't quite fast enough, though. As the elephant swung quickly down the streets with Harlan whipping papers left and right, the sky began to lighten. Instead of feeling he was riding a great dark shadow, Harlan could see the elephant beneath him more and more clearly. And if he could see him, anyone getting up early and looking out the window could see him, too.

Roger Mitchelson, a businessman on Harlan's paper route, had a very strange experience that morning. He arose before six o'clock, as he always did, showered, and selected the suit and tie he would wear for the day. After dressing, and carefully checking his watch to make sure he was on schedule, he went downstairs to make his breakfast. Breakfast was always the same for Mr. Mitchelson: a bowl of Toasty Wheats with skim milk and a cup of instant coffee. It always tasted awful, but Mr. Mitchelson didn't care; it was easy to make, and it didn't cost him any time. Being on schedule was very important to Mr. Mitchelson. He thought everything should be in its proper place, and every businessman should be in his office at the proper time.

On this particular morning, Mr. Mitchelson's wife came into the kitchen, as she always did, wearing her pink bathrobe and fluffy white slippers. She came into the kitchen to keep Mr. Mitchelson company, but, as usual, the moment she sat down across the table from him she fell asleep and started snoring.

So far, everything was the same as always. Mr. Mitchelson quickly shoveled in mouthfuls of Toasty Wheats in his mechanical way, occasionally chasing them with a swallow of oily-tasting coffee, and Mrs. Mitchelson snored along like a bass tuba in need of repair.

But then it happened. Glancing up from his breakfast and through the window behind Mrs. Mitchelson, Mr. Mitchelson saw an enormous gray shape moving past his house. The shape had a trunk on it, and great flappy ears. Behind it was a little tail. Strangest of all, there was a boy riding on it, a very small boy with bright red hair. The boy was smiling.

Suddenly, *Whack!* something hit the kitchen screen door. Mr. Mitchelson leaped up as though someone had set off a bomb. Mrs. Mitchelson's eyes opened sleepily and she asked, "What is it, dear?"

Mr. Mitchelson strode quickly to the door, and saw ... his newspaper. He looked out to the street, but it was empty now. He looked out there for a long time, and decided he'd better stop drinking coffee so early in the morning. The stuff was affecting his mind.

"Dear?" asked Mrs. Mitchelson.

"It was ... nothing," Mr. Mitchelson said. "Just the paper boy."

"Kooter," Mrs. Mitchelson said dreamily, and then she started snoring again.

Back at Harlan's house, Hannibal lifted Harlan down and eased into the garage just as the sun broke the horizon. Harlan followed him in and pulled the door shut.

"O.K.," Harlan said, "I've got to go to school now, but I'll be back this afternoon. Is there anything you need?"

"Cookies," Hannibal said.

"I'll get some on the way home from school," Harlan promised. "See you later, Hannibal."

The elephant didn't reply. He just stood there quietly in the dark garage.

"Hannibal," said Harlan, "is something wrong?"

"I don't want to go back," Hannibal said.

Harlan reached out and patted the rough, leathery hide of the elephant. "Don't worry, Hannibal," he said. "They won't find you here." Harlan left the garage and trotted up the street toward school.

When Harlan ran into class just before the bell, everyone was talking about the circus. "Hey," called Mickey Fungo, "here comes carrot-head. We didn't see you at the circus, Kooter."

"That's because I wasn't there, fungus," Harlan replied, settling into his seat. Mickey Fungo had never heard Harlan talk back before, and he didn't like it. His face swelled up like an angry red balloon. Monica Jeebers liked it, though. She covered her mouth with her hand and snickered.

"At least I got to see the elephants, Kooter," Mickey said, "unlike somebody I know."

Harlan just looked at him and smiled.

All that day, as he sat in the classroom and then raced around the playground, Harlan felt different, as though he had changed somehow. The truth was, he felt ... bigger. Of course, he couldn't have grown overnight — not much anyway. And examining his reflection in a window he saw at once that he wasn't any bigger than he had been the day before. But he *felt* bigger, and stronger, too. It wasn't until after school, on his way to get cookies for Hannibal, that Harlan realized what the feeling was: now he had a friend.

· 3 ·

HOW TO HIDE AN ELEPHANT

The next morning, Harlan and Hannibal left the house at the same early hour. They stopped a few blocks from the newspaper and Hannibal lifted Harlan down to the sidewalk.

"Try to be very quiet until I get back," Harlan said. "We don't want to attract any attention." He looked up at the elephant. "Did you hear what I said, Hannibal?"

The elephant's attention seemed to be somewhere else, though. His trunk was elevated and sniffing. "Cookies," he said softly.

"What?" asked Harlan, and then the faint scent of chocolate chip cookies drifted to his nose, too. "Oh," he said, "it's probably the bakery truck." Every morning, before it was light out, the truck from Hoffman's Bakery drove through Pine View, making deliveries at the school, the general store, and the Pine View Diner. Because the truck was already gone before most Pine

View residents got out of bed, Harlan was one of the few people who had actually seen it.

"Now, listen," Harlan said. "I'll be back with the papers in ten minutes. Stay right here, and don't let anybody see you, all right?"

"O.K.," Hannibal said.

Harlan hurried the rest of the way to the *Sentinel* on foot. He was rolling up his papers with Mr. Cheever when something on the front page caught his eye. It was still so dark that at first Harlan couldn't read anything, but then one of the workers inside the building opened the door and tossed out another stack. A bar of light from the open door fell across the newspaper in Harlan's hands, and he saw one word — ELEPHANT — before the door closed and the light was gone.

Harlan rushed to the door and opened it. Now the entire front page was bathed in light, and the headline made Harlan gasp. This is what it said:

ELEPHANT ESCAPES FROM CIRCUS

And underneath that headline was a smaller one:

SEARCH TO FOCUS ON PINE VIEW

The story went on to say this:

The Bumble Brothers' Circus has reported the loss of a young male elephant, a state police spokesman said today. The elephant, an African named Hanni-

33

bal, was discovered missing after the circus left Pine View, where it was performing last weekend.

The police believe the elephant is still roaming free in the Pine View area, and that is where they plan to concentrate their search efforts.

When contacted by the *Sentinel,* Peter Sarkonian, the animal's trainer, advised Pine View residents against approaching the elephant if they spot it.

"You don't know how powerful one of these things is," said Sarkonian. "I mean, if he sits on your car, forget it; you'll never drive it again. And another thing, don't leave any food around. I know this elephant; he'll do anything for a cookie."

Harlan would have kept reading, but Mr. Cheever had stepped over and was looking at him strangely. "Is everything all right, Harlan?" he asked.

Harlan looked up at Mr. Cheever. "Are the police really going to search Pine View for Hannibal — I mean, the elephant?"

Mr. Cheever glanced at the story on the front page. "Of course they will, Harlan. That elephant is a valuable animal."

Harlan swallowed quickly. "Do you think they'll find him?"

"I think it's pretty likely," Mr. Cheever said.

"What if ..." Harlan said carefully, "what if this elephant had a friend who helped him stay out of the way?"

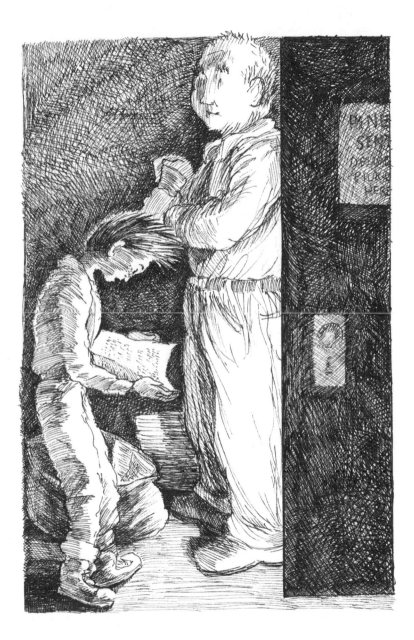

Mr. Cheever scratched his head. "Anybody with a friend has got a chance, I guess," he said. "Why, in a few days this whole thing could blow over and folks would go look somewhere else for that elephant. But I don't know where an elephant could find a friend like that around here."

Harlan was quiet after that. They finished packing up the rest of his papers and he hurried back to where he had left Hannibal. But when he got there, the elephant had vanished.

Harlan looked frantically in all directions. Where could Hannibal have gone? Suddenly, the rich, sweet smell of freshly baked chocolate chip cookies came to Harlan's nostrils again, and in that moment, he knew. Aiming for the smell, he dropped his newspapers in the street and started running.

Harlan caught sight of the bakery truck on Palm Street, after it had made its delivery at the school and was headed for the Pine View Diner. It was motoring along at a safe, low speed, and might have looked perfectly normal if it weren't for the elephant trotting along behind it. Hannibal had managed to get the truck's rear door open, and was rummaging around inside with his trunk. As Harlan watched, Hannibal pulled a bag of freshly baked rolls from the truck, examined it, and, discovering it contained no cookies, tossed it into the road. The trunk went back into the truck and came out with a loaf of bread, which it quickly threw aside before darting back inside to continue its search.

Harlan had almost overtaken the truck when he

made the mistake of looking behind Hannibal. What he saw made him stop running and put his hands to the sides of his head. For half a mile behind the elephant, a trail of muffins, rolls, croissants, bagels, cakes, and doughnuts was lying in the street, along with a dozen loaves of bread. Hannibal had somehow managed to find everything in the truck *but* the cookies. Harlan hesitated for a moment, unsure whether to start by picking everything up or to get the driver's attention first and then go back to clean up the road.

Before Harlan could decide what to do, Hannibal finally found the cookies. He pulled a bag of them out of the truck and trumpeted with happiness, causing the driver of the truck to look in his rearview mirror, scream, and drive off at top speed.

It took Harlan half an hour to pick up all the bakery goods and leave them at the Pine View Diner. Then he had to deliver his papers. Hannibal ate chocolate chip cookies along the route and all the way home, occasionally dropping one in the street. By the time Harlan got him safely hidden away in the garage, he was late for school.

That afternoon, when Harlan was walking home, he saw the policemen — Florida state troopers — driving slowly through Pine View in their patrol cars. They wore wide-brimmed hats and dark, reflective sunglasses that didn't let you see the eyes behind them. The troopers swiveled their heads slowly back and forth, looking everything over carefully. Harlan knew what they were after, of course. They were searching for Hannibal.

Harlan decided he couldn't just run home. It might make the troopers suspicious. So he walked home at a normal, everyday pace, whistling as he went. Actually, he only whistled part of the way, because he was so nervous his mouth went dry and then he couldn't anymore. When he got to his house he slipped quietly into the garage, where Hannibal was standing silently in the dark.

"*Ssssshhhhh,*" Harlan said.

"I didn't say anything," Hannibal said sensibly.

"I mean, be careful," Harlan said. "The police are out there looking for you."

Hannibal started trembling so hard that the garden tools on the walls of the garage began rattling loudly.

"Take it easy," Harlan said, and he patted the thick, gray hide of the elephant. "They'll never find you in here."

Just then, Harlan and Hannibal heard the squawk and static of a police car's radio. They heard the car's big engine, too, as it drove slowly down Harlan's street toward his house. As the car got closer and closer, Hannibal trembled more and more violently.

When the cruiser reached Harlan's driveway, it stopped. Harlan and Hannibal could hear the trooper calling in police codes on his radio, and the garbled, staticky replies. Hannibal started shaking so badly that the garden tools on the walls sounded as if somebody were rattling pots and pans in a kitchen. Harlan climbed up on a garbage can for height and hissed up to Hannibal's ear, "Stop it, Hannibal! Stop it right now!" And Hannibal stopped shaking.

They heard the car door shut as the trooper got out of the cruiser, and they heard his footsteps as he came up the driveway.

Harlan leaned forward and looked through a crack in the garage door. He saw the trooper stop, bend over, and pick something up. It was a chocolate chip cookie. Apparently the police knew that the elephant they were after was the cookie-eating kind. Harlan realized that Hannibal must have dropped this one on his way up the driveway.

Harlan held his breath as the trooper looked carefully around him. Hannibal was as still as a stone. Finally the trooper walked slowly down the driveway, got into the cruiser, and drove away.

"You see?" Harlan said. "Being in here is just like being invisible."

But Hannibal had already started shaking again.

Harlan was confident that he could keep Hannibal hidden. All the searching for the elephant seemed to be done during the day, and Hannibal only came out of the garage at night. Harlan was very careful to get his paper route done and Hannibal back in the garage before daybreak. But two days after the state police arrived in Pine View, Harlan was looking at a copy of the *Pine View Sentinel* when his eyes jumped wide open. This is what he read:

STATE INVESTIGATORS TO SEARCH
PINE VIEW BUILDINGS

State police officials, frustrated by their inability to find an elephant reported missing in Pine View, have decided to search all building structures in the town considered large enough to conceal such an animal.

"This is ridiculous," said Sergeant Alphonse Rodino, a state police spokesman. "An animal this big doesn't just disappear. I mean, what did he do, buy a bus ticket? He's hidden somewhere in this town, so what we're going to do is search all the hiding places. And I'll tell you something: this is one elephant who won't get away."

The police have decided to begin the building search today with all structures belonging to the town. Tomorrow, police personnel will begin searching all privately owned structures, including barns and garages. All such searches will depend on the consent of the owners, but the police expect full cooperation.

Harlan's heart thumped as he read the story. What would he do now? There was no way to keep the police out of the garage without making them suspicious. He had to think of somewhere else to move Hannibal, but where? That afternoon at school, he came up with the answer.

At Harlan's school was an old tool shed, bigger than Harlan's garage, where all the outdoor-maintenance equipment was stored. The school's big lawn mower was in there, along with shovels, rakes, ladders, hoses, sprinklers — everything a school could possibly need. Everything, that is, except an elephant. Well, Harlan thought, they didn't exactly need an elephant, but he was going to put one in there anyway.

That afternoon Harlan watched from his classroom window as the state police searched the school grounds. There were four of them, all wearing their uniforms and wide-brimmed hats. First they tried the gymnasium, and then they walked around to the tool shed. Mr. Simms, the janitor, unlocked it for them, and two of the troopers went into the shed with their flashlights. They came back out shaking their heads and all four of them left.

That's it, thought Harlan. Now that they've searched it, that's exactly the place.

The next morning Harlan and Hannibal finished the paper route before it was light. Then, instead of going home, Harlan rode the elephant to school.

The sky was just beginning to lighten when Hannibal lifted Harlan down in front of the equipment shed. Harlan started to reach for the door, and then realized he had forgotten something very important. The door had a big, shiny padlock on it.

"Uh-oh," groaned Harlan.

Hannibal laid his trunk on Harlan's shoulder. "What's the matter?" he asked.

"The door's locked," Harlan said.

"I can open it," Hannibal said, and before Harlan could reply, the elephant's trunk had slipped through the door's handle. Hannibal took a step back, set himself, and pulled.

The door started to bulge, and Harlan said, "Hannibal, wait—"

But it was too late. A second later, the whole door popped off the shed with a shriek of pulled nails and screws.

"Hannibal," cried Harlan, "you broke the door!"

"Sorry," Hannibal said quietly. "Do you want me to put it back on?"

Harlan sighed. "No," he said, "I'll do it. You just go on in."

Hannibal set the door down neatly against the side of the shed, and then silently glided inside.

"O.K.," Harlan said, "it's getting light out. I can't come back until it's dark again. Can you be very quiet until then?"

"Of course," Hannibal said.

"All right, then," Harlan said. "I'm going to put the door back on and go over and wait for school to start. I'll be back as soon as I can."

"Au revoir," Hannibal said.

"What?" asked Harlan.

"It's French," Hannibal said. "It means goodbye."

Harlan wondered how many elephants knew how to speak French. Maybe there were lots of them. He wanted to ask Hannibal but there wasn't any time. Instead, he huffed and puffed and strained to drag the door back into position. Just before he shut the door the last little crack he called inside. "Goodbye, Hannibal. See you tonight." Then he closed the door all the way and trotted over to the school.

· 4 ·

MICKEY MAKES A BIG MISTAKE

All that day, Harlan kept an eye on the tool shed. The grass was cut on the weekends, so Mr. Simms wouldn't have to go into the shed for the lawn mower until then. But what if he needed something else? Harlan's heart started jumping every time he saw the janitor walking around outside the school. All Mr. Simms had to do was open the shed door to get a rake or a shovel and it would be all over. After one look at Hannibal he'd probably scream and start running through the streets.

But Harlan's real worry was Hannibal himself. What if the elephant moved around and started knocking things over in there? Everybody in the school would hear the racket and come running. Or what if the elephant started singing to himself? The worst thing that Harlan could imagine was Hannibal falling asleep. All the elephant had to do was close his eyes, lean his shoulder against the wall, and the whole shed would tip over and collapse. That wouldn't bother Hannibal, of course. He'd just stand there in the wreckage, wondering what happened, or he'd wander off looking for cookies. Before it was even lunch time Harlan was so anxious he had a headache.

But as it turned out, no one went into the shed for anything, and Hannibal was very good about being quiet. Trouble, when it came, arrived from an entirely different direction.

Because Harlan was spending so much time looking out the window at the tool shed, Miss Honeycutt, his teacher, began spending time looking at *him*.

"Harlan," she said, in her high, reedy voice, "is there something out there more interesting than mathematics?"

"Oh, no, Ma'am," said Harlan. That wasn't quite true, but he knew when to keep his mouth shut.

"Now then, class," Miss Honeycutt said, "I'm stepping down to the office for a few moments. I expect you to behave yourselves until I get back."

The instant Miss Honeycutt closed the door behind her, Mickey Fungo began working on Harlan. "Kooter doesn't care about math," Mickey announced in a booming voice. "He's so poor he doesn't have anything to count."

Monica Jeebers liked that. She started in with her horrible giggle. Harlan stayed quiet. He had enough to worry about today without getting into a wrangle with Mickey Fungo.

Mickey turned his oversized body around in his chair so he could look back at Harlan with his big, leering face. "Isn't that right, carrot-head?"

Harlan folded his hands on the desk in front of him and smiled.

Mickey grinned wickedly. "You couldn't even go to the circus, could you, Kooter?"

Harlan wondered what Mickey's face would look like if he sat down on a barbecue, but he kept the question to himself.

"I'll bet you cried when you couldn't get in to see the elephants," Mickey sneered.

"I've got a pretty good idea what they look like," said Harlan, smiling pleasantly at Mickey. "I just imagine you with a trunk on your head."

Monica squealed in delight. The smile froze on Mickey's face, and then slowly fell off. He turned red, and then purple with rage. He seemed to swell up like a huge balloon, and then he rose up out of his chair and walked back to Harlan. He stood glowering over the smaller boy. "You take that back," he demanded hoarsely.

"Elephant," Harlan said quietly. "Elephant, elephant, elephant."

Mickey lifted his big, strong arms and reached for Harlan.

And at that moment, a long gray elephant trunk slipped in through the open window, circled around Mickey's waist, and whisked him outside. Just like

that. One moment the enormous boy was standing over Harlan, his face dark with rage, and the next moment he was gone.

Monica Jeebers started screaming. Everyone else in the class just sat there with their mouths open. Even Harlan looked surprised, but only for a moment. Then he jumped up and ran out of the room.

The whole class came pouring out of the little school behind Harlan. They really had no idea of where to go or what to do, so they just followed after him in a mob.

Harlan ran straight to the tool shed. The shed was still standing, but the door had been knocked down flat. Hannibal was gone.

Harlan turned around and yelled. "Mick-ey, where are you?"

Then all the children started milling around and shouting Mickey's name. The side door to the school burst open and Miss Honeycutt came running out. Harlan had never known that the old woman could move so fast. Mr. Mulligan, the stout little principal, was right behind her.

"Children," Miss Honeycutt shrieked, "what in heaven's name is going on?"

None of the children really knew, although Harlan had a pretty good idea, but Monica Jeebers started moaning and blubbering about an elephant trunk coming in through the window and carrying off Mickey Fungo.

"Monica, really," Miss Honeycutt said sharply. "An elephant in Pine View. What nonsense! And Mickey Fungo, of all people!" She snorted. "Even an elephant couldn't lift that boy."

Mr. Mulligan was jumping up and down in little hops. "Oh my goodness!" he cried. "Oh my goodness! It's true, Miss Honeycutt, it's true. Haven't you been reading the paper? There's an elephant loose in Pine View. He escaped from the circus. And now he's carried off one of the students!"

Mr. Mulligan fell down in a faint. Miss Honeycutt stamped her foot impatiently. "Oh, get up, Mulligan, you ninny. We've got to find the boy."

Mr. Mulligan sat up, woozily, but he didn't look as if he was going to be much help. Miss Honeycutt frowned and turned away from him. "All right, children, we're going to search for Mickey. I want you to spread out and look hard, but you're not to leave school property under any condition, is that clear?"

Everyone was very excited. "Yes, Miss Honeycutt," they chorused back.

But before anyone could move, they heard a high, wailing cry in the wind. "Heeelllppp!" At first nobody was sure where it came from. Then they heard it again. "Get me dooowwwnnn!"

At the far end of the playground stood a skinny, rickety-looking palm tree. It had been there ever since Harlan could remember, but he had never seen it looking like this before. Even though it had always swayed a lot when the wind was blowing, the rest of the time it had stood up fairly straight. But now it was bowed over in the middle, as though something immensely heavy was up among the tattered cluster of leaves at the top. Harlan squinted his eyes, looked closer, and saw there was something up there ... no, it was some*one.* Someone big enough to bend the whole tree over. It was ... Mickey Fungo!

"Heeelllppp!"

The class galloped down to the end of the playground and looked up to see Mickey hanging in the tree like some gigantic fruit. His face was red and he was clutching the palm fronds for dear life.

Miss Honeycutt arrived a moment after the class and glared up at the boy. "Mickey Fungo," she cried, "what are you doing up in that tree?"

Mickey's eyes were wide and staring. "It was," he gasped, "an elephant!"

"Mickey," Miss Honeycutt shrieked, "I will not tolerate such nonsense! Come down from there right now!"

Mickey's eyes widened as he looked at the ground far beneath him. "How?" he whimpered.

"The same way you got up," she yelled, "you ridiculous boy!"

"But the elephant put me here," he whimpered.

Miss Honeycutt stamped her foot, and stamped it again. In the center of each white cheek there was a deep flare of red. "Mickey!" she cried. "Down! Now!"

There was a long moment in which Mickey tried to decide which was worse, having Miss Honeycutt mad at him or falling out of the tree.

"I'll go get a ladder," Harlan said.

"Oh, very well," Miss Honeycutt said impatiently.

Some of the other children followed Harlan as he ran off to the shed. When he got there he realized that the ladder on the wall wasn't tall enough. Then he saw a coil of rope hanging at the far end of the shed and had an idea. He grabbed the rope and raced back to the tree with the others streaming after him.

"What's that for?" Miss Honeycutt asked, looking at the rope.

"Well," Harlan said, "I thought if we looped it over the top of the tree, just below the leaves, we could pull it down far enough for Mickey to jump off."

Miss Honeycutt nodded. "Very well, then — throw 'er over."

Harlan threw one end of the rope over the tree, then grabbed that same end and threw it over again, so the rope was wound around the tree like a little collar just below the leafy part. Half of the children grabbed one end of the rope and half grabbed the other.

"All right, class," Miss Honeycutt called, "pull!"

It wasn't easy, even for the whole class. Mickey's weight had already bent the tree over as far as it wanted to go, and now every inch more was hard work. It came down, though, bit by bit, as the whole class strained and pulled on the rope with all its might. And as the tree got closer to the ground, the fear started to leave Mickey's face.

Then, when it was still a good fifteen feet off the ground, the tree stopped bending. The children tried pulling even harder, but it just wouldn't budge. Mickey started looking scared again.

Miss Honeycutt looked at the class. "You think you're trying, but you're not," she said firmly. A boy behind Harlan groaned, but Miss Honeycutt ignored him. "You children are much stronger than you think," she said, "but you must ... put ... in ... more ... effort. Now, *pull!*"

Somehow they found the strength to pull harder. Every one of Harlan's classmates was making some ridiculous face or other, and if they could have looked at each other they would have burst out laughing and dropped the rope. But they were all concentrating too much for that. They hadn't worked so hard in all their lives. And it still wasn't enough. So they pulled even harder.

And the tree started bending again. Slowly, inch by inch, Mickey Fungo came down toward them. The tension in the rope was incredible. The tree was straining mightily in the other direction, and every time it gave another inch, a little hum would run down the rope and into the children's arms.

Soon Mickey was almost down. Harlan looked up to see how much farther there was to go, and saw Mickey staring right at him, from barely an arm's length away. Mickey didn't look scared at all anymore, Harlan noticed. In fact, he was starting to look mad again. He squinted at Harlan with hot, angry eyes, and his lip pulled back in a snarl. "This is all your fault," he said to Harlan. "And when I get out of this tree, carrot-head, you're going to be very sorry."

Harlan had heard Mickey say these things before; he wasn't very worried about it. And anyway the strain on the rope was so terrific it was all Harlan could do to keep his grip on it and keep pulling. He'd deal with Mickey when Mickey was on the ground.

But Mickey couldn't wait that long to deal with Harlan. Just before the top of the tree touched the ground, Mickey reached out to grab him.

Harlan jumped back—not much, just a little, but it was enough. He lost his grip on the rope, and before he could get it back again the rope was moving through his hands, and then, an instant later, through everybody else's. One more second and the friction made it so hot that everybody let go at once.

The tree snapped back upright like a catapult, flinging Mickey up in a great wide arc. The enormous boy howled as he sailed over the playground, over the hedge, over a bright strip of freshly mowed lawn, and into the deep end of the Havemeyers' swimming

pool. The children took off running, with Miss Honeycutt following along behind.

Mickey was still spluttering around in the water when the class got there, and then Mrs. Havemeyer came out of the house in a pink sunsuit with her little poodle on a leash. "Well, children," she said, "what a nice surprise. Would you like some lemonade?"

"Hooray!" cried the class, and until Miss Honeycutt arrived, no one paid any attention to Mickey Fungo.

The word went out quickly over all the police radios: not only was there a bull elephant still running loose in Pine View, now he was carrying off children. Dozens of additional police officers flooded Pine View. Units of the National Guard were quickly mobilized, and the Florida Fish and Game Department brought in a famous tracker, an old Seminole Indian named Claw. When Harlan walked home from school that afternoon, he saw that many of the troopers were now carrying rifles with telescopic sights. He shivered and hurried past them.

Hannibal didn't come home until after dark. And all that time Harlan waited nervously, wondering where the elephant was.

Just as Harlan was finishing dinner with his mom, he heard a tiny, delicate sound in the garage, and then a big *Ka-Bang* as a garbage can was knocked over.

"Oh, those raccoons!" Mrs. Kooter said.

"I'll get it, Mom," Harlan said, and he jumped up from the table and ran out the door.

It was Hannibal, of course. He had opened the garage and walked in, but forgotten to close the door behind him. So the garage was open to anyone who happened to look in, and if that someone happened to be a Florida state trooper with a flashlight, he would have seen the enormous rear end of an African bull elephant.

Harlan quickly pulled the door down. "Where have you been?" he asked Hannibal.

"In the swamp," answered the elephant.

"Was that you who stuck Mickey Fungo up in the tree?"

"Yes," Hannibal said quietly.

"Why?" Harlan asked. "Everything was going so well. In a little while the police would have gone away and left us alone. Now there's more of them than ever." Harlan didn't tell Hannibal about the National

Guard and the guns. "Why did you do it?" he asked.

"I thought he was going to hurt you," Hannibal said.

Harlan sighed. "Did you mean to frighten him, Hannibal?"

"No," said the elephant.

"You weren't going to mash him with your trunk or sit on him or anything?"

"Of course not," Hannibal said. "What would I do that for?"

"Because you were mad?"

Hannibal slowly shook his head. "I wasn't mad."

"Then why didn't you just set Mickey down in the playground?"

"Because," Hannibal said, "if he acts like a monkey, he should live in a tree."

Harlan was glad Hannibal hadn't wanted to hurt Mickey Fungo. Mickey wasn't Harlan's favorite person, but you couldn't have elephants going around sitting on people; it just wouldn't be right.

Harlan sighed and leaned against Hannibal's leg, which was like leaning against a big, gray tree. It felt safe and cozy in the little garage, but Harlan couldn't help thinking of all the men who were out in the streets of Pine View looking for them. Men with rifles and an Indian tracker named Claw.

"Hannibal," Harlan said, "we have some very big problems."

57

The next morning was like other mornings, quiet and peaceful, and as Harlan and Hannibal walked through the dark streets on their way to the *Sentinel,* it was hard to imagine that lots of people were searching for an elephant and whomever was hiding him.

As they passed by the Havemeyers' house, Hannibal suddenly slowed his stride.

"What is it?" Harlan asked.

Hannibal's trunk lifted and gingerly sniffed the air. "Water," he said.

"The Havemeyers' swimming pool," Harlan said. He had to smile when he remembered what Mickey Fungo had looked like splashing around in it the day before.

Hannibal came to a complete stop and sniffed some more.

"Come on," Harlan said, "we've got to get going."

Hannibal started moving again, but instead of continuing down the street he swerved toward the Havemeyers'.

"Hannibal," said Harlan, "what are you doing?"

Hannibal crunched through the Havemeyers' hedge and headed for the pool. "Let's go for a swim," he said.

The pool was dim and shadowy in the moonlight, and the windows of the Havemeyers' house seemed to watch them like enormous eyes.

"We can't go swimming in this pool," Harlan said. "It's not ours."

Hannibal kept right on going.

"Put me down," Harlan said crossly. "Right now."

Hannibal stopped at the edge of the pool and lifted Harlan down to the ground.

"Now, Hannibal," Harlan said, "let's get one thing straight—"

But before Harlan could finish, the elephant plunged into the pool. He did it gracefully enough that there wasn't much of a splash, but at the same time he filled up so much space that water flooded out of the pool in a little tide that surged around Harlan's ankles. For a moment the deck chairs at poolside lifted and tilted crazily before settling back down.

This was it, thought Harlan. They were really in trouble now. He wanted to tell Hannibal to get out of the pool this minute, but the elephant was nowhere to be seen. He was now completely under water.

Hannibal surfaced near Harlan's feet and shot a geyser of water into the air with his trunk.

Oh, brother, thought Harlan. "Well," he said, putting plenty of sarcasm in his voice, "how's the water?"

"Pretty good," said Hannibal. "Not enough mud." Then he submerged again.

At that moment, Mrs. Havemeyer's poodle came yapping around the corner of the house. Harlan frantically tried to hush the little animal, but the poodle ignored him. It went straight to the edge of the pool and yelped hysterically at the water. When Hannibal didn't appear, the dog grew even more excited and ran barking up and down the length of the pool. Soon a light came on in the house, and then an outside light that shone down on the pool. Oh, no, thought Harlan. Oh, no.

Then Mrs. Havemeyer came out of the house in her pink bathrobe. "What is it, Fifi, what's the matter?" she called. She caught sight of Harlan and stopped in her tracks. "Who is that?" she said. "Who's there?"

"Just me, Ma'am," answered Harlan. "Harlan Kooter, the paper boy."

"Oh," Mrs. Havemeyer said, but she sounded a little puzzled. "Isn't it a little early for that?"

Way too early, thought Harlan, but before he could say anything, he heard a deep gruff voice behind him.

"Is there any trouble here, Ma'am?"

Harlan turned around and saw a policeman walking across the lawn with a flashlight in his hand. Harlan's heart started thumping horribly in his chest, and for an instant he had a terrible vision of Hannibal and himself sharing a prison cell.

"Why, I don't think so," Mrs. Havemeyer said. She came to the pool, and so did the policeman, and they stood there together looking at Harlan.

"Who are you, son?" the policeman asked.

"Harlan Kooter," Harlan answered.

"The paper boy," added Mrs. Havemeyer.

"Isn't it a little early for delivering newspapers?" the policeman asked.

"Well," Harlan said, "I was just on my way to work. I wasn't actually delivering yet."

"I see," the policeman said, and leaned down close to Harlan. "Is this where you usually pick up your papers?"

"I'm sure Harlan was just taking a short cut," Mrs. Havemeyer said brightly. "Isn't that right, Harlan?"

The policeman didn't wait for Harlan's answer; instead he turned to look at Mrs. Havemeyer's poodle, which was still running up and down the pool and barking. "That animal certainly is excited," the policeman said. "I wonder what's got him spooked."

"Oh, Fifi's just high-strung," Mrs. Havemeyer said. "She'll calm down."

Harlan sneaked a quick look into the pool. Now that there was a light shining on the water, he could see a large dark shape moving around below the surface. His heart started thumping again and he quickly looked back at Mrs. Havemeyer and the policeman. How could they not notice?

The policeman studied the yapping dog for a moment and then turned back to Mrs. Havemeyer. "Does she often get this way?"

"Well," Mrs. Havemeyer said, "now that you mention it, no."

Mrs. Havemeyer and the policeman turned away from the pool while they talked, and as they did, the tip of an elephant trunk came out of the water and greedily sucked in the fresh morning air. Harlan was

horrified. He wanted to throw a bag over it or something—anything!—but there was nothing handy.

Fifi spotted the trunk and began jumping and spinning with new excitement, barking frantically all the while. The trunk sniffed delicately once or twice and then turned toward the dog, moving briskly through the water like the periscope of a submarine. Just before it reached the edge of the pool the trunk dipped silently below the surface.

Fifi stopped barking and tilted her head curiously. Her nose trembled as she slowly extended it over the pool.

The elephant trunk popped up and blasted her with water, submerging again as the little dog ran back around the house soaking wet and yipping in terror.

The policeman and Mrs. Havemeyer turned and looked at Harlan. "What was that noise?" the policeman asked.

"I, I . . . sneezed," answered Harlan.

The policeman stared at him and then looked toward the house, where Fifi was still yipping and yapping. "I'd better go see what she's barking at," he said. Mrs. Havemeyer followed him as he went around the house to investigate.

Hannibal chose that moment to clamber out of the pool. He stood there dripping and looking very contented. "I like a good swim," he said.

Harlan wanted to scream, but instead he just asked, "Would you like to deliver some papers now?"

"O.K.," said Hannibal. He picked Harlan up, set him on his back, and off they went.

· 5 ·

MONICA BLOWS THE WHISTLE

The policemen and soldiers searched through Pine View for two days and two nights. They turned every-thing in the town sideways and upside-down. They searched in the streets and they marched through the swamps. They looked here and there and everywhere, but they never found Hannibal the elephant. It didn't matter, though, because in the end, Monica Jeebers did it for them.

From the moment Mickey Fungo had been plucked from the classroom by the elephant trunk, Monica thought Harlan Kooter had been acting strangely. No one else noticed any change in him, but Monica sat at the desk right next to his, and she noticed a lot. She thought it was strange, for example, that after Mickey went out the window, Harlan was the first one outside looking for him. Monica had never seen Harlan lead anything in her whole life. The only thing she had ever seen him do was get sat on by Mickey Fungo and have his sandwiches stolen.

But that wasn't the only thing Monica noticed. After the class had fished Mickey out of the Havemeyers' swimming pool, all anybody wanted to talk about was the elephant. And whenever anyone suggested an idea for catching it and locking it up, Harlan cringed. At one point, he just put his hands over his ears and refused to listen. Nobody else saw it, they were all so busy chattering away, but Monica thought it was strange. It was as though Harlan was on the elephant's side.

Something else struck Monica as important, although she didn't know why. It was something about *when* the elephant had carried Mickey off. Something that had been happening just before. But what? All she remembered was that Mickey had started teasing Harlan, and then Harlan had teased him back, and then Mickey had gotten very mad, and then ... that was all. The elephant trunk had come in through the window, and Mickey was gone.

Monica thought about it all the time, but it took her two days to figure it out. It was as though she were putting a puzzle together in her head, and there was a piece missing. Round and round the puzzle went in her mind, until she thought she would shriek with frustration. But then, on Friday, the third day after Mickey had been dragged out the window and hung in the tree, she got it. It was a big surprise, even for Monica.

Miss Honeycutt was standing at the front of the

room, giving a history lesson, when Monica's eyes flashed in amazement. She shot up out of her seat with her hand clapped over her mouth, and turned to stare at Harlan as though he had just come back from the moon.

Miss Honeycutt stopped the lesson and glared. "Monica Jeebers," she demanded, "what are you looking at?"

Monica didn't even hear her. She slowly took her hand away from her mouth, but kept her eyes on Harlan, who was now staring back at her. "You know him," she whispered.

"Speak up, Monica," Miss Honeycutt called sharply. "I can't hear you."

But suddenly Monica was speaking very loudly. "You know that elephant, Harlan!" Then her mouth picked up speed and she began speaking more and more loudly until her voice sounded like a screeching tea kettle. "You know that elephant! That's why he

grabbed Mickey! Because you're friends! You and that elephant! That's why you covered your ears when everybody talked about catching him and putting him in a cage! Because you're friends! You're friends, you're friends, you're FRRIIIEEEEENNDDSSSSS!!!!!"

Everyone turned in their seats to look at Harlan, and from the look of horror on his face they all knew it was true.

"Harlan Kooter," cried Miss Honeycutt from the front of the room, "how could you?"

Everything happened very quickly after that. Miss Honeycutt ran to the office and screamed at Mr. Mulligan, and Mr. Mulligan telephoned the police, and the police turned on their sirens and their flashing lights and raced for Harlan's house. On the way they remembered to tell the National Guard where they were going, so everyone arrived at Harlan's at the same time. The police turned off the sirens but kept the lights flashing, and soldiers jumped out of the army trucks and surrounded the house.

When all the policemen and soldiers were in position, it suddenly grew very quiet. A beefy state police captain got out of one of the cruisers with a megaphone in his hand and took a few steps toward the house. Then he planted his feet and raised the megaphone to his mouth.

"All right in there," he thundered, "we've got this place surrounded!"

It so happened that Harlan's mother had gotten home from the Pine View Diner a few minutes before the police arrived. When the police captain yelled at the house through the megaphone, she came to the front door wearing her pink waitress's uniform.

"We know you've got the elephant," the captain barked, "so just come out quietly."

Harlan's mom opened the door, stepped out onto the lawn, and put her hands on her hips. She looked at the captain as though he were a bad little boy and spoke in a firm, clear voice. "Mister," she said, "you'd better have a very good reason for pointing that thing at me."

The mouths of some of the other policemen dropped open. They had never heard anyone speak that way to the captain before.

It didn't seem to shake the captain, though. He spoke again through the megaphone. "Is this the home of Harlan Kooter?"

Harlan's mom looked stunned for a moment, and then her eyes flashed wide open before quickly narrowing to hard, angry points. She took her hands off her hips and started walking toward the police captain.

"Now you listen to me, young man," she said, although the captain was almost old enough to be her father, "if you've done anything to my Harlan you are in very big trouble." Her voice had turned cold and steely, and although the captain was surrounded by his

69

fellow officers he blinked, twice, and swallowed. It had been a long time since anyone's mother had spoken to him in that voice, but he still knew what it meant. It meant business.

As Harlan's mom strode forward, the captain took a couple of steps back. He didn't mean to, especially in front of the other men, but before he could think about it he had already done it.

Harlan's mom might have walked right through the captain, or over him, but just then the officer in command of the soldiers stepped up to talk to her. He was a calm, gray-haired man and he spoke with careful respect.

"Your boy's fine, Ma'am, just fine. He's over at the Pine View school right now, all safe and sound."

Harlan's mother stopped and looked the man over. "Well, then," she said, "what's all this about?"

"Ma'am," the soldier said, "we have reason to believe there's a runaway elephant hidden on the premises."

Harlan's mother stared at him for a moment, and then started to laugh. "An elephant? Here?" She laughed some more, looked at all the other soldiers and policemen, and laughed even harder. "Where would we hide him, in the living room? It's hardly big enough for Harlan and me." Her laughter settled down to delighted giggles. "Maybe in the kitchen? The refrigerator?"

The men surrounding the house looked a little

sheepish now. Some of them were studying the ground in front of them and others were shuffling their feet.

Harlan's mom was still giggling. She stepped back toward the house, stopping in front of the garage. "Maybe he's in here, men, right along with the garden tools." She stooped down, and with a triumphant whoop of laughter flung open the garage door.

And there stood Hannibal the elephant.

Hannibal blinked in the bright sunlight. "Hello, Mrs. Kooter," he said quietly.

Harlan's mother stared at Hannibal. Her mouth came open, and then it closed again. Finally she was able to speak. "Who ... what are you doing here?"

But before Hannibal could answer, the police captain began shouting orders. "All right, men. Let's get him out of there. Bring those chains over now."

The soldiers raced up first and prodded Hannibal out of the garage with their rifles. As soon as they had him standing in the driveway, the policemen attached heavy chains to his legs. It all took less than a minute.

A big tractor trailer truck had pulled up in front of

the house, and the soldiers prodded Hannibal until he started walking toward it. His head hung low and his whole body seemed to sag. It was hard for him to move with the heavy chains on his legs. They made a clanking, dragging noise as he walked slowly along.

The truck driver opened the back of the trailer and dropped a ramp to the street. Hannibal stopped at the bottom of it and the soldiers started poking him with their guns again. He walked up the ramp and the door swung shut behind him.

Harlan came hurrying up the sidewalk as the driver climbed up into the cab, but before he could call out Hannibal's name or say goodbye, the truck pulled away and was gone.

Once they had captured Hannibal and forced him into the truck, the police were faced with a whole new problem they had not thought of before—where to keep an African bull elephant until the circus could come to collect him. The Bumble Brothers had been notified immediately of Hannibal's capture, but the circus was now traveling through Texas, and it would be days before they could send a truck for him.

No one in Pine View was willing to have Hannibal in their garage or barn, which left only the public buildings as possibilities. Someone suggested putting Hannibal in the firehouse, but that would mean parking the town's only fire engine outside, and the firemen weren't going to stand for *that*. It was finally

agreed that the best place for him would be the gymnasium of the Pine View School. And that's where
they put him.

Harlan was suspended from school for a week. The
principal told Harlan it was only because nobody had
gotten hurt that they were letting him come back to
school at all. Some people in town thought he should
have been suspended forever, or better yet, put in jail.
Harlan's mother told him she was deeply disappointed
in him, and if another circus ever came to town, she
was going to lock him in his room until it was gone.

Having everybody mad at him was pretty bad, but
the worst part for Harlan was not knowing what they
were doing to Hannibal. He had tried to explain to
people how gentle Hannibal was, and how he never
would have hurt Mickey Fungo or anyone else, but nobody would listen. They had made up their minds that
Hannibal was a dangerous rogue elephant, and that
was that.

On his third day at home, Harlan couldn't stand it
any longer. He had to see Hannibal. He slipped out of
the house and started walking to school.

It was early afternoon, a bright sunny day, and
Harlan moved quickly along the streets in his high-
topped sneakers.

The school was quiet when he reached it. Recess
was over and there was no one on the playground.

Harlan walked softly around to the back of the
gymnasium. No one in the school noticed him, but

that didn't surprise Harlan. It was one of the advantages of being small; if you walked quietly, people often didn't even see you.

Harlan reached the back door of the gym, opened it carefully, and stepped inside. What he saw almost broke his heart.

In the center of the gym was Hannibal. He looked tired and sad. Around each leg he wore a band of iron, and attached to each band was a heavy chain that ran across the floor and was bolted into a wall. Hannibal could hardly move. He was so dejected that he didn't even look up when Harlan walked in.

Harlan went slowly over to Hannibal, and for a while he didn't say a word. Then he reached out and patted the elephant's trunk. "Hello, Hannibal."

At first he didn't think the elephant had heard him. Then Hannibal slowly moved his ears forward. "Harlan?" he asked. He sounded miserable.

"Yes," Harlan said, "it's me."

The elephant didn't say anything more, he just lifted his trunk and laid it on Harlan's shoulder. They stood that way for a long time, two friends with a problem they didn't know how to solve.

Finally Harlan said, "I have to go now, Hannibal, before my mom gets home."

The elephant took his trunk off Harlan's shoulder and his head drooped down again.

"I just wanted to stop by and see you," Harlan said,

trying to sound cheerful, "because you're my very best friend."

Hannibal was looking at the floor. He didn't say anything at all.

"Goodbye," Harlan said. Then he walked to the door. He didn't turn around to look at Hannibal before he left. He couldn't stand to see him that way.

As Harlan walked home, the day was still sunny and bright. He looked up at the sky and couldn't understand it. If there were no clouds above him, and if it wasn't raining, then why did everything look so blurry and why were his cheeks so wet?

· 6 ·

HURRICANE ROSCOE COMES To TOWN

The next morning, Harlan woke up even earlier than usual. His window was open, but the curtains were absolutely still. There was no breeze at all coming off the ocean, and the air in his room felt curiously ... full, somehow. It was as though something invisible but powerful was being carried in it, something like an electrical charge. Harlan suddenly had the sense that something immense was going to happen. He didn't know why he felt that way, exactly, but it had something to do with the strangeness of the air. Harlan climbed out of bed, dressed, and went outside.

As he walked along, Harlan noticed something very odd. Usually by the time he was outside and under way in the morning, birds were already stirring and singing in the trees. But on this morning there were no birds singing at all. It was as though they were all hiding from something. But that was silly, Harlan thought. What would they be afraid of?

When Harlan got to the *Sentinel* he learned why the birds weren't singing.

Mr. Cheever was waiting for him outside the back door of the building, stacking the papers as they came off the press. "This may be the last paper you deliver for a few days," he said as Harlan walked up.

Harlan blinked at him. "Is this because of my elephant?" he asked.

Mr. Cheever smiled. "No, no, the *Sentinel* isn't here to pass judgment on you or your elephant, Harlan. We're just here to report the news. Know what the news is this morning?"

Harlan shook his head.

"Big storm heading this way," Mr. Cheever said. "BIG. A hurricane. Started up south of Bermuda."

Mr. Cheever took Harlan inside to the lighted press room and held up a newspaper for him to read.

HURRICANE ROSCOE TO HIT PINE VIEW TONIGHT

A tropical storm that formed approximately five hundred miles southeast of Bermuda earlier this week has developed into a full-scale hurricane and is heading directly for Pine View. The National Weather Service, which named the hurricane Roscoe, believes it will reach the Florida coast by nightfall.

The Pine View School is closed for the duration of the storm. Florida authorities are urging residents to take precautions and to be prepared for possible evacuation.

Harlan's eyes widened as he read the story. He had never seen a hurricane, not in person anyway. He had seen them on the news, though, and the thought of one roaring through Pine View was exciting.

"This time tomorrow there's going to be a lot of wind and water around here," Mr. Cheever said. "We wouldn't risk your safety in a storm like this."

"Roscoe," whispered Harlan, looking down at the paper.

"That's right," Mr. Cheever said, "Hurricane Roscoe. And he looks like a doozie." Mr. Cheever laid a hand on Harlan's shoulder. "I'm sorry about what happened to your elephant, son. You can understand why people were so worried, though, can't you?"

Harlan nodded. "But he isn't a bully, like everybody says he is. He's a very polite elephant." Except when there are cookies around, Harlan might have added, but he didn't think Mr. Cheever would understand.

"Well, it's too bad you don't have him now," Mr. Cheever said. "An elephant could be very helpful in a big storm like this; you never know when you'll need something heavy to be lifted out of the way. There are going to be a lot of fallen trees around this town by midnight, believe me."

Harlan loaded his papers into his bag and hurried off to his route. He wondered how many people knew a storm was on the way. Probably not a lot. Almost everybody in town was still sleeping.

As he hurried along, Harlan was filled with antici-
pation. A real storm was coming to Pine View. A hurricane! Big enough to blow trees over! If only he had
someone to share it with, thought Harlan. If only he
had Hannibal.

All that day, the little town of Pine View prepared for
the approaching storm. Anything that might be blown
or floated away was carried inside or lashed down se-
curely. Windows had boards nailed over them so the
wind couldn't smash them to pieces, and rows of
sandbags were laid down so the rising water wouldn't
flood the town. People felt sure that when Hurricane
Roscoe hit that night, the town would be ready.

But the storm didn't arrive that night. It reached
Pine View that afternoon.

At four o'clock the sky suddenly darkened. The air
began to stir, and then flow in a steady breeze. Standing in the yard in front of his house, Harlan knew this
was the first breath of the approaching storm.

The ocean scent in Pine View grew sharper as spray
from the rising waves drifted into town. Little sand
trails began twisting across the roads as the wind
skimmed sand from the beach and cast it inland. The
people of Pine View looked out to sea and began to
hurry their preparations. Was this it? they wondered.

By five o'clock it had become so dark in Pine View
that all the lights in town were on. There was a high
moan in the wind by then, and in the distance could be

heard the sound of the dark crashing waves that grew taller and more powerful with every passing moment. Although it had not yet begun to rain, the streets grew wet from the sea spray carried in by the wind, and the pavement glistened under the headlights of passing cars.

Harlan and his mother were inside their little cracker-box house, listening to a weather report on the radio. The full force of the storm would be hitting the coast shortly, the announcer said, and just then the wind outside the house jumped higher and began to howl. They could hear it race eagerly through the town, carrying seawater with it. Branches started tearing loose from trees, and some of them rattled and thumped against the house.

Then the rain came, as though someone had turned on a faucet. One moment there was only the wind, and the next the drops were rattling against the sides of the house like hail. The radio, which had sounded crisp and clear, quickly faded into garbled static.

Harlan looked at his mom. "Wow," he said quietly.

She smiled at him. "We don't need the radio to tell us there's a storm, do we?"

Harlan shook his head, but he was worried about the radio. Without it, how would they get emergency instructions from the police? He went into the kitchen, picked up the telephone, and listened. He didn't hear anything.

"Mom," he said, "the phone's not working."

And then the lights went out.

Harlan heard his heart thumping loudly in the darkness as Hurricane Roscoe screamed and howled around him. His mom lit some candles and the living room quickly filled with a comforting glow. Harlan's heartbeat slowly returned to normal and he walked out of the kitchen and sat down on the sofa.

Now that the power was out, the radio wasn't even making static. Its silence made the wind and rain seem a lot louder. Or maybe, thought Harlan, they *were* louder. Maybe the storm would just get louder and stronger until the little house was lifted off its foundations and flung away like a leaf in the wind. He shivered as he thought about it. The idea of a big storm had sounded like a lot of fun that morning, but now as he listened to Hurricane Roscoe tear and claw at the house, he wasn't so sure.

They sat listening to the storm until it was time for Harlan to go to bed. Then he took a candle down the hall to his room and set it on his nightstand. After he had crawled under his warm, snug covers, he blew out the candle. It felt safe being there in bed.

As he lay there, though, Harlan began to think about Hannibal. It had to be awfully scary, he thought, for the elephant to be all alone in the gymnasium on a night like this. He wondered if anybody had even told him that a storm was coming. Well, thought Harlan, at least Hannibal was inside.

But then Harlan thought of something else. The school gymnasium was built on ground level. If the water rose just a few inches, it would flood the gym. Harlan thought the water had to have risen more than that by now. He opened the drawer by his bed and pulled out the flashlight he had stowed there. Then he snapped it on and directed the beam out the window by his bed.

The water was high, all right. It was swirling over the driveway in a swiftly moving flood. It was hard to tell how deep it was, but Harlan was sure it was already flooding the gym. And the storm had only just begun. It was supposed to go on all night and into tomorrow.

They had forgotten Hannibal; Harlan was sure of it. He thought of his friend trapped in the gym as the water rose around him, trying to get away as it went up to his knees, then to his stomach, then up to his chest....

Harlan knew what he had to do. He had to go and set Hannibal free. But the sound of the wind frightened him. He didn't want to go out there.

A moment later he clenched his fists and spoke into the darkness. "I'm coming, Hannibal. Just hang on, O.K., buddy?" Then he took a deep breath and climbed out of bed.

In Harlan's closet was a pair of battered old rubber boots and a bright yellow rain slicker. He put them on. The boots were a good snug fit, but the slicker was an old one of his mom's and he had to roll up the sleeves halfway. There was also a yellow rain hat in the closet, and he took that down and pulled it over his ears. Now he was ready.

Harlan slipped the flashlight into the pocket of his slicker. He walked to his window in the darkness and felt for the latch with his hands. He found it, turned it open, and lifted the window.

The sound of the storm jumped to a high-pitched scream. The wind seemed to reach for Harlan and tear at him, as though it wanted to drag him from the house and into the raging storm. It shifted back and forth with lightning quickness, and every time it did, a stinging lash of water struck Harlan across the face. He only stood there for a moment, but that was enough time for a voice inside him to say, "Don't do it, Harlan, don't go out there."

But he had already made up his mind. He climbed out the window and hung from the sill with both hands. Then with one hand he reached up and closed the window. He hung on for a moment, and then he let go and dropped.

He landed on both feet with a splash and steadied himself against the wind. He pulled the flashlight from his pocket and snapped it on. The water was halfway to the tops of his boots! That meant the whole town was under a foot of water!

Harlan snapped the light off and put it back in his pocket. He didn't want his mom to see it and drag him back inside.

When he reached the sidewalk Harlan turned right and headed for school. The wind grabbed and pulled at him, and the rain pelted against him. Before he had gone three blocks the water had seeped down the collar of his slicker and his shirt was soaking wet.

But he was making progress. He was moving along slowly but steadily, and he knew if he just kept going he would make it.

By the time he got to the edge of the school playground, Harlan was drenched and his muscles ached from pushing against the wind. But he was still on his feet. The water was rising, though. Now it was almost to the top of his boots.

He started across the playground, and in a few minutes he made it to the back door of the gymnasium. He reached for the handle and then he heard Hannibal inside. The elephant was trumpeting in fear.

So it was true. They had left Hannibal behind, not caring if he drowned in the storm. Well, *I'm* here, thought Harlan, and that's just not going to happen. He tugged on the door but the surging water pressed it shut.

Another trumpeted yell came from Hannibal.

Harlan put one foot on the wall next to the door and hauled with all his might. The door came open a few inches and Harlan slipped inside.

The water inside the gym was just as high as it was outside. It must be seeping in under the doors, Harlan thought. Hannibal trumpeted again and Harlan snapped on his flashlight and called, "It's me, Hannibal! It's Harlan!"

Hannibal quieted when he heard Harlan's voice and he waited for Harlan to wade to him through the water.

The rain on the roof and the wind outside made such a racket that he had to shout even when he got close to Hannibal. "We'll get you out of here," he said, "don't worry."

"I don't think so," Hannibal said. "These chains are heavy."

Harlan couldn't see the chains around Hannibal's

ankles because they were under the water. But he remembered them. They were big and strong-looking. He remembered they were attached to Hannibal's legs by heavy iron bands and ran from Hannibal to the walls of the gym.

"I'm going to go have a look at the other ends of these chains," Harlan told Hannibal. The elephant made a low, mournful sound when Harlan moved away from him.

Following the chains, Harlan discovered that each one was attached to an iron ring bolted to the wall. Harlan tugged on one of them. It felt very firm. It wouldn't be easy getting it loose, but as far as Harlan could see, it was their only chance. He waded back through the rising water to the elephant.

"Have you tried pulling on the chains?" he asked.

"Of course," Hannibal said.

Harlan felt his heart sink. But he tried to sound cheerful for Hannibal's sake. "Well, instead of pulling on all of them at once, we're going to concentrate on just one right now. O.K.?"

"All right," Hannibal said. He didn't sound convinced.

"We'll start with your right front leg," Harlan said. Hannibal nodded.

"Here we go," Harlan said. "Ready ... PULL!"

Harlan felt the great strength of the elephant gather, and then half the chain became visible above

the water as Hannibal pulled it taut. It stayed that way
for a few moments and then the elephant gasped and
relaxed.

"Did you feel anything?" Harlan asked. "Did it
give at all?"

The elephant slowly shook his enormous head. He
looked very, very dejected.

Harlan felt his own spirits starting to fail him. He
had come so far, all this way through the terrible
storm, and now it seemed that Hannibal wouldn't
escape anyway.

But then Harlan remembered Miss Honeycutt, and
how everybody in the class had almost given up on
getting Mickey Fungo down from the tree until she
had gotten them to pull on the rope harder than they
ever believed they could.

Harlan looked at his friend. "Listen, Hannibal," he said. "Elephants are the strongest animals in the world. You know why you can't pull that chain out of the wall? Because you think you can't. You tell yourself it's impossible. Well, let me tell you something, Hannibal. THAT'S NOT TRUE! And I'll tell you something else. You and I are in this together. If you don't get out, I'm not getting out either."

Hannibal lifted his head when he heard that. "You can't stay here, Harlan; you'll drown."

Harlan folded his arms. "You're my best friend, Hannibal. Unless you pull those chains out, I'm staying." And he meant it, too. He wouldn't desert Hannibal. Not ever.

Hannibal blinked at him. "I'll try, Harlan."

"You'd better," Harlan said. "It's getting awfully wet in here. Ready?"

Hannibal nodded.

"O.K., then," Harlan said. "PULL!"

Hannibal's enormous body seemed to flex, and then the chain snapped taught again. Hannibal began to breathe heavily as he pulled and strained, but the chain remained fastened to the wall.

"I ... can't," gasped Hannibal.

"You can't," Harlan said, "BECAUSE YOU'RE NOT PULLING! Now, pull, Hannibal, pull with everything you've got! Pull the wall out! Pull down the whole world!"

Hannibal seemed to settle down into the water a

little more than before, and he raised his trunk and trumpeted a wild, furious call. And then, he pulled . . . and pulled . . . and pulled. Suddenly, a squeaking nose came from the wall, and then a groaning scream as the iron ring loosened . . . loosened, loosened . . . and pulled free.

Harlan was jumping up and down in the water. "*Ya-hoo! Whee-ha!* What an elephant! The greatest in the world!"

One by one they worked on the other three rings, until Hannibal was free. The chains were still attached to Hannibal's legs, but now he could at least escape the rising water.

Harlan unlatched the double doors at the far end of the gym. He couldn't budge them, because of the water pressing against them, but Hannibal lowered his head and pushed them open. And suddenly, Harlan and Hannibal were out in the storm.

The noise was tremendous. The wind and rain ripped and tore at them like claws. Harlan looked up at the elephant and yelled, "Can you find some high ground where you'll be safe from the flood, Hannibal?"

"Of course," answered the elephant, who was suddenly very calm and sure of himself.

"We can try to get the chains off after the storm," Harlan said.

"Good idea," Hannibal said.

"O.K.," Harlan said. "I've got to get home before the water gets any higher."

"I'd better give you a ride," Hannibal said.

"I'll be fine," Harlan said. "You take care of yourself, all right?"

The elephant nodded and Harlan hugged his leg. "Good night," shouted Harlan above the noise of the storm. "I'll see you later."

"Good night, Harlan," called the elephant.

Harlan waded off across the playground. The rain was so thick that after he had gone a few yards, Hannibal couldn't see him anymore.

· 7 ·

ONLY AN ELEPHANT
CAN SAVE THEM

When Harlan awakened the next morning, the wind and rain were still lashing fiercely about his house. The world outside his window looked dim and gray and very, very wet. He climbed out of bed and saw the sticks and branches and mud he had brought in with him when he climbed back in his window the night before. He could just imagine what his mother would say when she saw *that*.

He walked down the hall to the living room and found his mom asleep on the sofa. He got a blanket from the hall closet and covered her with it. The candles had long since burned out, and the room looked pale and colorless in the gray stormlight filtering through the windows.

Harlan was devouring a muffin at the kitchen table when he heard a sharp rapping at the front door. He opened the door and saw a policeman in a fluorescent orange raincoat. Water was streaming down from the policeman's hat, and his nose and cheeks were red from the whipping wind. "Is this the Kooter residence?" he asked. He had to shout it to be heard above the storm.

"Yes, sir," Harlan said, "but we don't have any more elephants."

The policeman looked at him sharply. "I don't care about any elephants, son, I just want you to get ready to move. The water's getting too high for you to stay. How many people are living in this house?"

"Two," Harlan said.

"I want both of you ready to move in ten minutes," the policeman said. "Can you do that, son?"

"Yes, sir," Harlan said. "I think so."

"Well, get a move on," the policeman said. "I'll be back soon." He turned away from the door and struggled down the steps with the wind snatching at his orange raincoat. When the policeman reached the walk in front of the house, Harlan saw that the water was up to his knees.

Harlan shut the door and turned to tell his mother what the policeman had said, but she was already bustling around gathering up things they'd need when they left the house. Harlan ran and got his raincoat, his boots, his toothbrush, and his quilt. He brought them out to the living room and put them on the couch.

Harlan's mom was in the kitchen, putting some food in a shopping bag. "Is that everything you need?" she called.

"I think so," Harlan said, and then he suddenly darted back down the hall to his room. He pulled his baseball mitt from the shelf in his closet and hurried out to the living room with it. He didn't think he'd be playing any baseball for a while — in fact, he had never gotten on a team. But if the house washed away he didn't want to lose his mitt, because things could always change.

Harlan had just pulled on his old rubber boots and yellow rain slicker when a loud knocking sounded at the door again. Harlan's mom smiled at him. "Well, kiddo, here we go."

Harlan grinned at her and opened the door. Now there were three policemen outside the house. The one who had been there before was back, and at the bottom of the steps were two more, both wearing the same bright orange raincoats and standing at either end of an aluminum skiff. Harlan's eyes widened when he saw it. The water was deep enough now to float a boat in!

Already in the skiff were the Smiths, the old couple who lived next door. The wind was whipping their hair around, and they were drenched by the rain. They waved at Harlan as he came down the steps with his quilt and toothbrush and baseball mitt all stuffed together in a shopping bag.

The policeman helped Harlan settle in next to the Smiths, and then his mom after him. "Did you bring anything special?" Mr. Smith called to Harlan over the wind.

Harlan nodded. "My baseball mitt."

Mr. Smith smiled down at him. "Good choice." The old man held up a black umbrella that was twisted and broken. "I brought this along to keep the missis dry," he said, "but the wind caught hold of it."

Mrs. Smith managed to smile at Harlan, even though she was soaking wet and leaving her house behind.

The policemen pulled the skiff away from the steps and guided it over the underwater lawn to the sidewalk. The four passengers looked at each other as the boat was pushed out from the curb into the deeper stream. And then, with the policemen walking alongside, they floated on down the street.

As the skiff glided along, Harlan began to feel as though he were in another town, one he had never seen before. The streets had vanished beneath the wind-whipped water, and all the houses seemed to be floating free of the earth beneath them. Many of the trees he was used to passing on his way to school were gone, and others reached into the air like clutching hands. Street signs stuck out of the water to mark nothing at all.

Of course, Harlan and his companions weren't the only people out that morning. Through the driving gray rain Harlan could see other boats moving over the submerged streets, some of them being led by orange-coated policemen, some of them not. Behind a row of houses to Harlan's left, he saw two people furiously paddling a canoe.

As they left his neighborhood, Harlan asked one of the policemen where they were going.

"Over to the firehouse," the officer said. "The second floor is nice and dry."

"Are lots of people already there?" Harlan asked.

"Not as many as we'd like," the policeman said. "There was one street down at the lower end of town that's almost completely underwater — all the houses, I mean. We didn't find out about it until this morning. Everybody who lived there climbed onto the roof of the *Sentinel* to get above the water, and now we don't know how we're going to get them down."

The *Sentinel* building came into view a few minutes later. It wasn't even a quarter of a mile from where Harlan's boat was passing, but Harlan could see how much deeper the water was in that part of town. Some of the one-story houses there were completely underwater, with only a chimney or a television antenna sticking up from the dark surface. The *Sentinel* wasn't a tall building, but because it stood on higher ground than the rest of the neighborhood, it was not yet submerged.

The real spectacle was on the *Sentinel* roof, where Harlan could see a small group of people. These must

have been the ones the policeman told him about, the ones who had left their flooded homes and climbed up there in the middle of the night. The water surged and crashed against the red brick building beneath them.

Harlan guessed there were about twelve people on that roof, and every one of them looked cold, miserable, and frightened. He could see why it would be difficult to rescue them. The roof of the building was still too high above the water line for the police to get to it. Any boat coming close to the building would be taken by a wave and smashed against the brick walls.

As Harlan watched, a huge wave surged up to the building and broke against the edge of the roof, showering the people there with icy seawater. If the water rose much higher, they would all be swept away.

Harlan looked carefully through the wind and rain to see if he recognized anyone on top of the building. The way they huddled together kept him from seeing their faces, until one of them, someone big, stepped away from the group to look fearfully at the rising water. It was Mickey, Mickey Fungo! A girl with pigtails came over to stand beside him and look at the water, too. She took one look at the angry, rising waves, and began to howl. That was Monica Jeebers! Harlan wondered for a moment what two kids from his class were doing on the roof of the *Sentinel,* and then he remembered that both of them lived in that part of town.

It was terrible to look at the people up there, all of them waiting for the big wave that would sweep them out to sea.

"Isn't there any way to get them down?" Harlan

asked one of the policemen.

"Right now we're stymied, son," the officer answered. "We just can't figure out how to get close to them."

Harlan could see the problem. In order to get them off the roof you'd need . . . suddenly, Harlan knew exactly what you'd need to rescue a bunch of people stranded on a rooftop. You'd need an elephant! An elephant tall enough to wade through the deep water, and equipped with a trunk strong enough to pluck people from the roof and carry them to safety. An elephant just like Hannibal! And in that moment, Harlan made his decision.

He turned to his mother and said, "Don't worry, Mom, I'll be back."

"What are you talking about, Harlan?" his mother asked.

"I know how to get those people off that roof," Harlan said, "and I'm going to do it."

"How—?" was all his mother had time to say, and then Harlan jumped out of the boat. Mrs. Kooter screamed.

The water was so cold Harlan was shocked by it. His eyes jumped wide open and he yelled, but he didn't get back in the boat. Instead, he turned and struck out for the school. One of the policemen grabbed for him, but Harlan was too quick and small to catch.

"Harlan!" yelled Mrs. Kooter. "Where are you going?"

"See you later, Mom!" he called back. "I'm going to get Hannibal!"

His mother yelled at him again, and told him to get back in the boat this instant, but in a few moments he had vanished into the storm.

As Harlan struggled through the icy water and gray swirling rain, he realized he didn't know where to find Hannibal. But the last place he had seen him was at the school, so that's where he headed. He wished he hadn't scared his mother by jumping out of the boat, but there was nothing else he could have done.

The water was much higher than it had been the night before. It was up to Harlan's waist now. The coldness seemed to squeeze his legs and take the strength out of them. But he kept pushing on. Tree branches swept by him on the water's surface, and so did other things — furniture cushions, a basketball, a breakfast menu from the Pine View Diner.

Finally the school came in sight. The rain fluttered around the little building like a long, gray veil. Harlan looked hopefully across the playground, but there was no elephant in sight. Well, of course not, he said to himself; you told him to go somewhere else and find higher ground.

Harlan slogged on toward the school anyway, not

knowing what else to do. The wind was howling so loudly that he didn't think anyone would hear him, but he started yelling anyway.

"HANNIBAL! . . . HEY, HANNIBAL!" called Harlan. His voice sounded tiny in the screaming wind.

Harlan realized he was getting tired. As he pushed on across the playground it got harder and harder to move his legs through the icy water. He wondered how much longer he could keep going.

When he reached the gym the doors were still open, but Hannibal was gone. He called the elephant again, but the sound was whisked away by the wind.

Harlan began to feel as though the rain was battering him, beating him down. The water kept rising all around him, making it more and more difficult to move. He thought he'd better find some higher ground himself now.

He considered climbing up on the school roof, but he knew that he would only end up being trapped there. He left the school and began moving through the streets again.

The surging water was moving up to Harlan's chest. He called Hannibal's name again and again, but his voice was losing its strength. He was feeling very tired. "Hannibal," he called again, but this time it came out as a feeble croak.

Then, as Harlan came to a half-submerged street sign, he stumbled off a curb that was hidden under the surging flood. He pitched face first into the icy water and was carried away on its surface like a spinning leaf. Struggling as he was swept along, he was able to turn onto his back and gasp for air. It came into his mouth with a spray of rain. Then he was flipped over onto his stomach again. Everything was darkness and cold turbulent water. He tried to turn over so he could breathe, but the water was too strong for him. His lungs began to ache for fresh air. He struggled some more, but he seemed to have less and less strength, and the water seemed more and more powerful. He made up his mind that he would never give up, that he would keep fighting the water no matter what, but that didn't seem to matter. His floating body seemed to race along faster and faster, and the world in his mind began to dim, as though a light was fading out.

"I will not give up," Harlan thought to himself. "I will not . . ." and then he forgot what he was thinking. He tried to remember, but it was very hard. Everything was turning dark.

Just before the light went out, Harlan became aware that something was circling his waist, something strong, like a rope. And then, in one sudden moment, he was pulled from the water. He opened his mouth and the breath exploded out of him. He breathed in the fresh rain-washed air. It tasted so good! Soon his mind began to clear. Where was he? he wondered. How had he gotten out of the water?

Harlan looked down at the rope around his waist and saw that it wasn't a rope at all. It was a thick gray elephant trunk. Hannibal! Hannibal had found him!

· 8 ·

HANNIBAL TO THE RESCUE

Hannibal was holding Harlan up in the air and examining him. Harlan's chest was heaving and his face was pale.

"Are you all right, Harlan?" the elephant asked.

Harlan nodded and kept breathing. Hannibal swung him up over his head and onto his back. Harlan lay limply with his face pressed against the elephant's neck and his arms and legs draped on both sides. Hannibal let him catch his breath and then asked him, "Do you want me to take you home, Harlan?"

"No," Harlan said, "we've got to save Mickey Fungo."

Hannibal thought about that. "Is he up in a tree again?"

"He's trapped on the roof of the *Sentinel* building," Harlan said. "Pretty soon the waves are going to drag him off and out to sea."

"Oh," Hannibal said. "I hope he can swim."

"It doesn't matter if he can swim," Harlan said. "This is a hurricane. Nobody could swim in this."

"Oh," said Hannibal.

"Monica Jeebers is up there, too," Harlan said, "and a whole bunch of other people. Only an elephant can save them."

"Well, we'd better get going," Hannibal said.

"Wait," said Harlan before the elephant could move. "I want you to know, Hannibal, that if we help these people, you could get caught again, and sent back to the circus."

Harlan felt the elephant take a deep breath and let it out slowly.

"O.K.," Hannibal said. "Thanks for telling me."

"You'll still go?" Harlan asked.

"We have to," said Hannibal.

And so they moved off through the storm together, the great gray elephant and the small red-haired boy perched on his back. It was slow going even for Hannibal. He had to put his head down and strain against the immense force of the hurricane. His ears flapped and rippled in the wind.

Harlan had to cling to the elephant's neck with all his strength just to hold on. The wind was rising again, whipping the rain against his face with a stinging fury. He knew that if he lost his grip for an instant the wind would pluck him off Hannibal's back and carry him off into the storm. Feeling Hannibal beneath him was

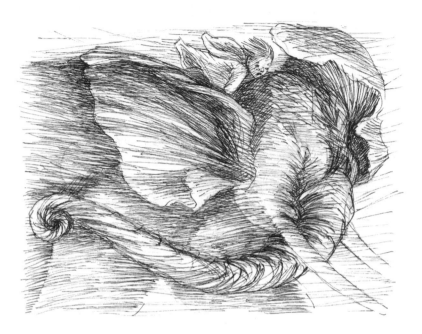

comforting, though. Hannibal was so big and strong that Harlan didn't think anything could ever knock him over. The elephant just put his head down and moved steadily through the storm. Every now and then the wind would hit Hannibal broadside and he'd slow for a moment. But he never stopped moving forward.

The water was high. As they got closer to the *Sentinel*, it rose steadily up Hannibal's legs. Harlan looked down at it and clung even tighter to the elephant's neck.

Soon the water reached Hannibal's belly. It kept

rising until the broad expanse of his back looked like a movable gray island.

Harlan's eyes widened as he looked at the water. He called out loudly, "Are we going to make it, Hannibal?"

"Of course," the elephant said.

Up ahead of the *Sentinel* building, the water had risen so high that almost every wave was breaking on the edge of the roof and flinging a sheet of water over the people trapped there. It wouldn't be long before they were swept away.

Harlan saw Mickey Fungo up there. The boy was turning frantically in every direction, looking for a way to escape. Then Mickey saw the elephant with Harlan perched on his back. He raised his hand to point at them and began to shout. The other people on the roof came over to look. They stood in a wet, huddled clump and watched as the elephant and the red-haired boy approached.

When Harlan and Hannibal reached the *Sentinel* building, the water crashed and swirled around them. Hannibal shuddered from the force of it. Mickey stood at the edge of the roof, staring down at them with his mouth open in surprise. The other people up there looked as astonished as he did. There were twelve of them altogether, children and grown-ups, including two huge people that Harlan thought must be Mrs. and Mr. Fungo. The group looked cold and ragged, some with soggy blankets around their shoulders, some just shivering in their rain-soaked clothes. None of them said anything, not even Monica Jeebers, who looked down at Harlan and Hannibal with amazement.

Harlan cupped his hands and called up to Mickey Fungo. "Come on, Mickey, we're going to get you out of here."

Hannibal raised his trunk to pick the boy up, but Mickey backed away from the edge of the roof with frightened eyes. "You're not going to get me, Kooter!"

Hannibal looked up at Mickey and sighed. "That boy is awfully silly," he said to no one in particular.

The other people on the roof began backing away with Mickey.

"That's the one," Mickey told them. "That's the elephant who kidnapped me. He's crazy mean."

Hannibal sighed again, "Oh, boy," he said.

Harlan cupped his hands and tried once more. "Mickey," he yelled above the wind, "we don't want to hurt you. We want to get you down from there."

Mickey kept moving away. "Get out of here, Kooter," he yelled. "Get lost." The rest of the people on the roof moved back with him.

Suddenly Monica Jeebers left the others and ran to the edge of the roof. "I'll go," she called. "Come on, Harlan, take me!"

Hannibal's long gray trunk darted up and plucked her delicately from the roof. He set her down gently on his back, just behind Harlan.

Mrs. Jeebers, a skinny woman with wet tangled
hair, broke away from the others and ran to the edge of
the roof. "Monica," she screamed, and stretched out
her arms, "what are you doing down there? Come
back here at once!"

"Get her, too," Harlan said, and Hannibal's trunk
streaked up like lightning and wrapped itself around
Mrs. Jeeber's waist. The wild-eyed woman screamed
as though she were being murdered, and then Hannibal hauled her down and set her on his back. When
Hannibal released her and she found herself sitting
behind her daughter, she quieted down.

"Let's take these two first," Harlan said. "We'll
come back for the others."

"O.K.," Hannibal said. "Where will we take them?"

"The firehouse," Harlan said.

Hannibal nodded and they started fighting their way through the wind and rain.

As Hannibal moved away from the *Sentinel*, Monica Jeeber's mother clung to Monica, Monica clung to Harlan, and Harlan clung to Hannibal for dear life. The wind whipped and tore at them, the rain continued to soak them, but gradually the water below them grew more shallow as they approached the upper part of town. Along the way they encountered a number of people in different sorts of boats, all of whom stopped whatever they were doing to stare at Hannibal and his passengers.

When they reached Pine View's town square, Harlan thought it looked like a gigantic swimming pool. The water wasn't nearly as high as it was around the *Sentinel* building, but the whole square was flooded. The first floor of the red brick firehouse was awash in storm water, and the Pine View Diner looked like a half-submerged submarine.

As Hannibal strode into the shallow water in the square, the chains around his legs became visible again. Harlan had forgotten about them. He realized how hard it must be for the elephant to drag them through the water.

There were rescue workers in the square, including some policemen in their bright orange raincoats, and when the elephant walked by with his three riders perched on his back, their mouths fell open in amazement.

Suddenly, an upstairs window at the firehouse was flung open and Harlan's mother put her head out through it. "Harlan!" she yelled. "Where have you been? What are you doing on that elephant?"

"It's O.K., Mom," Harlan called back. "Hannibal and I are helping those people on top of the *Sentinel* building. Here's two of them now."

Mrs. Kooter would have kept shouting, but Hannibal circled Monica Jeebers with his trunk and held her up to the window. Mrs. Kooter put her arms around the cold, shivering girl and carried her inside. By the time Harlan's mother came back to the window Hannibal was holding up Mrs. Jeebers. Mrs. Kooter helped her inside, too, and when she returned to the window this time, Hannibal and Harlan had turned away and were headed back to the *Sentinel* for more passengers.

"Harlan!" Mrs. Kooter yelled. "Come back here at once!"

"We've got to get the rest of them, Mom," Harlan called back. "Don't worry, we'll be fine." And he and Hannibal kept on going.

But before they could leave the town square, a group of firemen blocked their way. "Hold it, you two," said a tall fireman standing in front of the others.

"Uh-oh," Hannibal said.

Harlan started to plead with them, to explain that they couldn't lock up Hannibal now, not when he was on a rescue mission, but the tall fireman said, "Don't worry, son, we're on your side."

Another fireman came sloshing through the water with a big hammer and a chisel. He bent down and struck off Hannibal's chains, one after another. When he was done he stepped back out of the way.

"Good luck to you both," the tall fireman said. "We're all counting on you."

Harlan and Hannibal hurried off into the storm. It was easier for Hannibal to move now, but the storm was wilder than ever.

Returning to the *Sentinel,* Harlan was alarmed to see how much farther the water had risen. Even between waves it had almost reached the roof.

By now the people on the roof were ready to leave. Only Mickey Fungo and his enormous parents were holding back. One by one, Hannibal transferred people from the roof to his back, four this time, and then they headed for the firehouse as the wind howled and screamed around them.

When Harlan and Hannibal reached the firehouse again, a number of firemen were outside to help with the passengers. As soon as they were safely inside, the elephant turned around and headed back to the *Sentinel.* This trip went smoothly, too, and when it was over the only people left were Mickey Fungo and his parents.

The three Fungos were huddled together at the edge of the roof when Harlan and Hannibal returned. Mickey's parents were trying to talk to him, but he was shaking his head. He looked at Harlan and yelled, "Forget it, Kooter, I'm not going."

Just then a wave crashed against the edge of the roof, drenching the Fungos and knocking down Mickey's mom. When the wave came down the far side of the building, it almost swept Harlan off Hannibal.

Harlan shook his head to clear it and yelled up, "Come on, Mickey, there isn't much time!"

But Mickey wouldn't budge. "I'm not getting on that elephant," he said. "I know what he wants to do to me."

"He wants to rescue you, Mickey," Harlan said. "*I* want to rescue you."

Boom! Another wave crashed against the building and soaked the Fungos.

There just isn't any more time, thought Harlan. "You'd better put me up there," he told Hannibal.

"On the roof?" asked Hannibal. "Why?"

"I've got to talk him down."

Hannibal sighed. "I wish you wouldn't do this." But he circled Harlan with his trunk and lifted him up to the roof.

"Look, Mickey," Harlan said after Hannibal had released him, "you can't stay up here. In about five minutes the water is going to carry you off the roof anyhow, so you might as well come with us."

Mickey started to cry. "I know what that elephant wants to do to me. He did it once already. And you probably told him to do it, Kooter; I know you're out to get me." Mickey stopped talking then, but he kept on blubbering. Harlan noticed that the overgrown boy's nose was running.

Mickey's parents tried to reason with him. "I don't think that's so, son," Mrs. Fungo said. "Harlan seems like a perfectly nice boy."

"Let's give it a try, Mickey," Mr. Fungo said gently. "Wouldn't you like to go for an elephant ride?"

Mickey just kept snuffling and moaning.

"I'll tell you what, Mickey," said Harlan. "If you promise not to eat any more of my sandwiches, or call me carrot-head ever again, I'll make sure nothing happens to you on the way to the firehouse."

Mickey stopped snuffling for a moment and looked at Harlan. "Really?" he asked. "You promise?"

Harlan nodded solemnly. "I promise."

Ka-Boom! Another wave smashed against the building, crested the edge of the roof, and knocked them all down. The four of them tumbled around in the frothing water for a few moments before they were able to get to their feet.

"Let's go!" Harlan cried to the Fungos. He ran to the edge of the roof and called down to the waiting elephant. "O.K., Hannibal!"

Instantly, the elephant's trunk snaked up and wrapped itself around Harlan's waist. A moment later, Harlan was settling gently onto Hannibal's back.

Hannibal looked up at the enormous Fungo family waiting at the edge of the roof and said to Harlan, "This isn't going to be easy."

"You can do it," Harlan said.

The first Fungo to come down was Mickey's mom. Hannibal seemed to strain a little as he brought her down, but he was able to handle her gently and gracefully. Next came Mickey, who wasn't much heavier, and then came Mickey's dad. He was the hardest. Hannibal could barely reach his trunk around the man. But he braced himself and eased the massive Mr. Fungo down slowly, settling him on his back just behind Mickey. Then they were ready to go.

They began moving away from the *Sentinel* building just in time. The waves were crashing furiously about the roof now, which was quickly disappearing beneath the water. The flood was up to Hannibal's mouth and he had to breathe through his trunk, which he kept elevated above his head. All of Hannibal's passengers clung together as the wind and rain screamed around them.

Gradually, as Hannibal pushed on, the water

seemed to recede around them, and Harlan knew they were moving up to higher ground. As they slowly climbed out of the deepest water, Harlan looked back and saw the *Sentinel* building totally swallowed by the water. One moment the roof of the building was visible, and the next a wave crashed down on it and it was gone beneath the milling surface. And this time, it stayed under. Harlan faced forward again and shuddered.

It seemed that every fireman in town was outside in the rain when Hannibal got to the square with his passengers, as well as most of the police. Everybody was cheering. Horns were going off and sirens were blowing. Even Mickey Fungo looked happy. He waved to the crowd and everybody waved back.

The Fungos were quickly passed in through the firehouse window, and then everybody else hurried for shelter. The firemen had fixed up a place for Hannibal in the garage where they usually kept the fire engine, and they had rigged a pump that bailed all the water out of the building.

And so, with everyone snug and dry and under shelter, the people of Pine View waited as Hurricane Roscoe tore through their little town. And late that night, in the deep darkness just before dawn, Roscoe moved on.

· 9 ·

HOME SWEET AFRICA

On a bright, sunny day, shortly after the hurricane had left Pine View, a stranger drove a car into town. He was a big handsome man with a ruby in one ear. His name was Pierre Lambeau, and he was captain of a ship called the *African Star.*

As Captain Lambeau drove through the little town, he could see the effects of the storm. Some of Pine View's biggest trees had been pulled up by the roots and thrown down again. Others had simply snapped in two. Many of the little houses were covered with mud or tipped over on one side. Water was everywhere — puddles as big as small ponds lay shining in the sun.

When Captain Lambeau reached the town square he parked his car and walked directly to the firehouse. A fireman let him in and showed him to the living quarters upstairs. The main room was crowded, as every fireman in town was in attendance, along with Harlan and many other Pine View citizens.

Captain Lambeau sat down and nodded to all the people staring at him. "Maybe someone can tell me now," he said, "why it was so important that I come here."

Fire Chief Flanagan spoke up first. Flanagan was a short, stout man, mostly bald but with a fringe of iron gray hair around the sides of his head. He was smoking a big cigar. "We have a passenger we'd like you to take to Africa," he said. "A friend of ours."

Captain Lambeau looked around at all the expectant faces and smiled. His smile was strong and bright and it warmed the room like sunshine.

"If he is your friend," Captain Lambeau said, "why don't you save him time and buy him an airplane ticket? He will get to Africa much faster that way."

Chief Flanagan glanced at the other firemen and quietly said, "Certain people are looking for him."

Captain Lambeau was still smiling. "Of course they are. He is African, your friend?"

"That's right," Flanagan said. "He's from Kenya. We want you to get him to Africa and then put him on a train for home."

"Your friend has a passport?" asked Captain Lambeau.

"Not exactly," Flanagan said. "He's an elephant."

Captain Lambeau's eyes widened for a moment and then he threw his head back and laughed and laughed.

The firemen looked at one another. Maybe it would be useless to try to get Hannibal back to Africa, some of them thought. Maybe they had found the wrong captain, thought some of the others. Harlan was worried.

When Captain Lambeau stopped laughing, he smiled at them again. "And now your elephant friend wants to go home, but some people want him to stay here, in a zoo, perhaps?"

"A circus," Flanagan said.

Captain Lambeau nodded. "And how did you come to be such good friends with this elephant?"

"He saved a lot of people in the storm," Flanagan said, "and we decided he deserves to go home." The little fireman puffed fiercely on his cigar. "I'll tell you one thing," he growled, "nobody's putting him in a cage again."

"That's right," rumbled some of the other firemen.

Captain Lambeau gazed at them steadily. "I have a place for your elephant on my ship," he said. "I'll take him back home for you."

A small cheer went up, but then Flanagan asked, "How do we know your ship is the right one? This is no ordinary elephant, you know."

"And the *African Star* is no ordinary ship, " Captain Lambeau said. "She has come through many storms, some of them as big as the one you have just seen. Trust in me and the *African Star*. We will get your friend home."

A small cloud rose as Chief Flanagan drew thoughtfully on his cigar. He stared at Captain Lambeau for a while, then took the cigar from his mouth and smiled. "All right, Captain," he said. "The *African Star* it is."

Now everybody cheered loudly. Harlan stood on his chair and yelled, "Hooray!"

When the noise had quieted down, the captain gave them directions to his ship. Then he said, "Bring your friend tonight after dark. We sail tomorrow on the morning tide. If your friend is not there, I am sorry, but we cannot wait." Then the captain got up, said goodbye, and left the firehouse.

After Captain Lambeau had gone, the room was very quiet. Some time went by without anybody saying anything. Chief Flanagan was the first to speak. He had been puffing on his cigar, but now he lifted it from his mouth and cleared his throat. "You know," he said, in his rough gravelly voice, "I'm going to miss that elephant."

Harlan and Hannibal were by themselves in the garage of the firehouse. The big red fire engine was parked outside.

"Well," Harlan said, "I guess this is it."

Hannibal didn't reply for a moment. Then he said, "This is what?"

"I mean," said Harlan, "this is goodbye."

"You're not coming to Africa?" asked the elephant.

"My mom wouldn't like that very much," Harlan said.

"Oh," Hannibal said. After a while he laid his trunk on Harlan's shoulder. "You could come and visit me sometime."

Harlan's face brightened. "Do you really think so?"

"Why not?" Hannibal said.

"You'll have to get someone to write me a letter when you get home, so I'll know where you are," said Harlan.

"O.K.," Hannibal said.

Neither of them spoke for a while. Then Harlan said, "I'm glad I met you, Hannibal. You're the best friend I ever had."

Hannibal felt around Harlan's face with his trunk. "Now I'll be your African friend," he said. "And I'll be waiting for you to come for a visit."

The door opened and Chief Flanagan came in. "O.K., fellas, it's time to go. We've got the truck waiting outside."

The firemen outside opened the garage door, and Harlan and Hannibal walked out into the town square. The night was fresh and cool, and a full silver moon hung over Pine View. Almost everyone in town wanted to go to Coral Harbor to see Hannibal off, and all over the square were cars filled with people. The big truck that would carry Harlan and Hannibal also waited in the square, its motor rumbling softly.

As Harlan and Hannibal walked to the truck, Mickey Fungo stepped out of the shadows. He looked big and pale in the moonlight. Harlan and Hannibal stopped and looked at him.

"I just wanted to say," Mickey said softly, looking down at his feet, "thank you. Thank you for saving my life, and for saving my mom and dad, too." Then he took a breath and spoke even more quietly. "If I acted like a jerk, I'm sorry."

Hannibal reached out with his trunk and gently tickled Mickey's ear. "Forget it, Mickey."

Harlan smiled. "Do you want to come with us to Coral Harbor, Mickey?"

Mickey looked up in surprise. "You mean it?"

"Sure, I do," Harlan said. "Come on."

Mickey cracked a big grin. "You're O.K., Harlan."

He held out his hand and Harlan shook it.

Someone behind Harlan said, "What about me?" He turned around and saw Monica Jeebers. "Can I come, too?" Monica asked.

"Of course you can," Harlan said.

The four of them walked to the truck and then up the ramp and inside. The boards enclosing the back of the truck were spaced widely apart, and they could see out between them. There was no top overhead, and the moon shone down on the elephant and his companions, making them look all silvery.

The ramp came up, the door was shut, and someone called out, "Ready!"

All the waiting cars started their engines and turned on their headlights, and one by one they drove out of the square. Hannibal and his friends watched them go, and then it was their turn. The big truck lurched as it started to move, and everybody grabbed Hannibal for support. The truck picked up speed, swung around the square, and took the south road out of town.

From inside the truck, Harlan could see the cars from Pine View making a string of lights ahead of them on the road. Turning to look the other way, he saw another line of lights following along behind.

The road to Coral Harbor ran along the shore, and on this night the beaches were white and the ocean was wide and shining beneath the moon. Hannibal put his trunk out the side of the truck so he could better smell the ocean.

Up ahead, Harlan saw the red, blinking lights as the leading cars in the caravan signaled and turned off the coast road into Coral Harbor. The big truck growled as it was downshifted, and then it, too, turned off the main road.

Once they began driving through the streets of Coral Harbor, the ocean smells began to turn to harbor smells. The smells of fish, and motor oil, and old wooden boats drifted into the back of the truck. Hannibal kept his trunk out and savored them all.

They drove slowly through the narrow streets, and then emerged at the harbor. It was a good-sized one, running for more than two miles in a wide curve. At the far end, where the water was deepest, a row of ships nestled against the docks. Among them was the *African Star*.

The caravan moved carefully along the edge of the harbor toward the ships. When they had almost reached the end, a man with a lantern jumped up on the running board of the truck. "Captain says, 'Everything must go quietly,' " Harlan heard him whisper.

The man rode with them the rest of the way, directing them where to park when they reached the ship. The truck came to a stop, the rear door was opened, and the ramp was lowered. Hannibal and his friends walked out of the truck.

The *African Star* was much bigger up close than it had looked from the other side of the harbor. It loomed above them like a great long wall, darkened except for a small green light on one side of her bridge and a red light on the other. They could barely make out the shape of Captain Lambeau, standing quietly at the rail above them. He slowly waved a hand in greeting, and Harlan waved back.

A small crowd of firemen and policemen and Pine View townspeople gathered around Hannibal, gently patting him and wishing him good luck. Monica Jeebers started crying quietly, and Hannibal put his trunk around her shoulders. Then the man with the lantern pointed the way to the loading ramp, and Harlan and Hannibal walked toward it.

The man with the lantern took Harlan's arm. "I am sorry, my friend. Captain says only the elephant on board."

Harlan turned and looked at Hannibal, and then hugged the elephant's tree trunk of a leg. Losing your

best friend wasn't much fun, he thought. Then he felt Hannibal's trunk mussing up his hair and tickling the back of his neck and he started laughing. He pulled his face away from Hannibal's leg.

"I'll miss you," Harlan said.

"Hurry up and come to Africa," the elephant said. "I'll be waiting for you."

Then Hannibal followed the man with the lantern up the ramp.

Harlan stood waiting in the darkness with Mickey Fungo and Monica Jeebers. Mickey had his arm

around Harlan's shoulders and Monica was holding Harlan's hand tightly. Harlan felt sad and happy at the same time.

"Well," said one of the firemen standing nearby, "it won't be long now. It's almost dawn."

And just then, the ropes holding the *African Star* to the dock were freed and pulled up to her deck. The people on the dock heard orders being given on the ship, and then she slowly backed away into the harbor. As she turned to head for the harbor entrance, the sky began to lighten.

After that it quickly grew brighter in the harbor, and Harlan could see that the *African Star* wasn't black as he had thought, but a beautiful deep green. Her smokestack was a bright Christmas red. A puff of smoke emerged from the stack and she began to make headway.

Harlan looked around him in the pale new light, and for the first time he realized just how many people had come with them to Coral Harbor. It must have been everybody in Pine View!

"Look," someone called, "look on the ship!"

Over on the *African Star,* a large, dark shape was standing by the stern rail.

"It has to be him," said a woman in the crowd, and then, as though to dispel any doubts, Hannibal trumpeted across the water to the people of Pine View. The whole mob ran down to the end of the dock, jumping and waving and cheering wildly. The *African Star* gave a long blast on her horn.

On the eastern horizon, the sun rose from the sea a dazzling orange red and began to climb the sky. The ship sounded her horn again, and Hannibal the elephant sailed forth from the harbor, toward Africa and the morning sun.

14784

F
HAR

Harvey, Dean

The secret elephant
of Harlan Kooter

$13.45

DATE			